U0088360

電話英語一本通

1 2 3
4 5 6
7 8 9
* 0 #

MP3

張瑜凌◆編著

Making a phone call

【序文】
從 Hello 開始英文溝通！

「用英文溝通」有多重要？多年來，在全球村概念的發酵下，沒有到不了的國度、也沒有無法溝通的語言，當「英語」已經成為全球化溝通的語言工具的第一選擇時，你不得不承認，此時，該是開始學習英語的時機了！

「網路」及「電話」是能夠跨越地區性阻隔的溝通工具，但是在某些網路不盛行的地方，就只有電話能夠對外溝通。相形之下，「電話溝通」就成為跨越國界地區的重要選擇了！

該何時準備好用英語和外籍人士溝通呢？就從這一刻開始，因為你永遠不知道當電話響起的那一剎那，來電者到底是不是用英語和你溝通的。

「電話英語一本通」收錄最實用、最好記的電話英語實用例句，以及配合職場需求的情境語錄，再附上由外籍教師逐句導讀的MP3 光碟，讓您能夠充分利用瑣碎的時間逐句練習，熟記最道地的電話英語。

Part 1 電話英文溝通技巧

Part 2 電話英文〔會話篇〕

Chapter 1 打電話

Chapter 2 接起電話

Chapter 3 確認來電者身份

Chapter 10 和電話留言相關的用語

Chapter 11 回電話

Chapter 12 電話打不通

Chapter 19 電話相關用語

Chapter 20 電信服務

Part 3 職場情境短語

Chapter 1 辦公室電話用語

Chapter 2 秘書電話用語

Chapter 3 總機人員電話用語

Chapter 4 警察電話用語

Chapter 5 航空公司人員電話用語

Chapter 6 旅館櫃臺人員電話用語

Part 4 基本句型

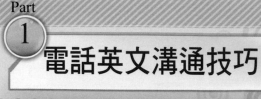

Part 1

電話英文溝通技巧

Chapter 1
何謂「電話溝通」

　　人際之間的溝通（communication）有許多種方式，最普遍、也最為一般人所熟悉的溝通方法就是「語言溝通模式」。而「使用相同的語言」則是語言溝通的基本要件，此模式套用在英文的學習過程中不難發現，在學習英文時，要以「能夠正確而有效溝通」作為學習英文的原則。

　　語言的溝通管道除了彼此面對面之外，另一種經常使用的溝通管道便是「電話」（telephone）。在「地球是平的」（The World Is Flat）這本書中提到，全世界沒有圍籬，只要有能力跨越，就能擁有全世界。在地球是平的概念下，足以擔任連結全球平台的工具之一就是「電話」，而串連起聯絡溝通的語言就是「英文」。

　　藉由電話所形成的溝通模式，更是英文學習過程中的重要議題。為什麼呢？因為透過面對面溝通，可以藉由肢體語言輔助溝通的進行，但是電話溝通則必須完全仰賴對方聲調及語句來作為判斷的標的。

○ 人際溝通的技巧

　　那麼何謂「有效的溝通」模式呢？簡單來說，從電話鈴聲響起（或撥出電話）的那一刻起，直到道別掛斷電話為止，中間的過程沒有出錯並能達到正確無誤地傳達彼此的訊息時，就是一個有效的溝通過程。而這個有效的溝通過程也能夠為你建立良好的人際關係網路。

無論是在進行面對面或是利用電話作為溝通管道，「聆聽」（listen）皆扮演著重要的角色。尤其是透過電話所進行的溝通方式，因為我們看不見對方的表情變化，但是透過聆聽的過程，感受對方的語調起伏，進而判斷對方的情緒狀態，便能使這一條電話溝通管道通暢無阻。

○ 增加電話溝通的信心

大多數的商業往來必須在電話中進行，此時便會產生相關的人際溝通的行為，從一開始接到電話的哈囉，一直到掛斷電話時所說的再見，都是一段電話溝通的行進過程。

在地球村的概念發酵之下，商業活動與人際關係之間的建立，不再侷限在與本國人進行，人們足以藉由電話進行跨越種族、陸地、洲際的藩籬，進行大規模的溝通行為。

若想做好電話溝通，就必須熟悉一些英文的基本句型的用法（詳見P305）。如此一來，才能夠在兼顧電話禮儀（Telephone Manners）與電話技巧（Telephone Skills），建立起電話溝通的信心。

Chapter 2
電話溝通的藝術

　　「電話溝通的藝術」並不是一門高深的學問，但是有一些重要的基本禮儀卻容易被一般人所忽略，反而造成一段不愉快的電話溝通過程，因此正確的「電話溝通的藝術」是每個人都必須重新學習與重視的。

　　「電話溝通」最重要的兩大架構是「打電話」與「接電話」的過程，只要能順利地掌握這兩個過程，將使您成功地贏得人際關係。

○ 電話溝通的基本禮儀

　　有哪些基本的電話溝通的禮儀要特別注意的呢？分成三個基本架構：

一、打電話的禮儀

　　（一）正確的電話號碼：首先，一定要注意的，當然就是撥打正確的電話號碼（dial the right number）。也許會有人說，「既然撥打這個電話，當然就表示我撥打的號碼是正確的」，但是你是否曾經犯了這個錯誤：連自己撥打出去的電話號碼都不確定自己能否順利地再覆誦一遍？那是因為你記不住這個電話號碼。當可能撥錯電話而對方質問你撥打的號碼時，可能連你自己都支支吾吾難以回答吧！撥打電話出去時，請先再一次確認所要撥打的電話號碼吧！

　　（二）對所有接電話者保持一貫的基本禮貌：對
於你經常打的電話，像是某些工作伙伴、朋友，相關
可能接電話者的身份最好都一併瞭解一番。因為你的
受話方有可能無法接電話，而由其他人接電話（an-
swer the phone），對於代接電話的人，也請不要忘
記尊稱對方身份的禮儀（詳見P38）。

　　除非你確認對方的專線電話（direct line）絕對
不會有其他人代接，否則撥打電話前，請有心理準
備，可能是一位非預期的人所代接的電話。

　　（三）電話接通時的寒暄：電話接通後，不論撥
打電話的時間早晚，請一定要遵守寒暄、打招呼的基
本禮貌，以下的說法都是最常見的用語：

【例　如】
▶ Good morning.
　早安！
▶ Good afternoon.
　午安！
▶ Good evening.
　晚安！
▶ Hi.
　嗨！
▶ Hello.
　哈囉！

以上打電話的寒暄禮儀，也適用在你接電話時，

應該要遵守的電話禮儀。

二、接電話的禮儀

當你接起電話，發現自己不是對方要找的人，那麼就應該幫對方轉接電話，這時請務必遵守請對方稍等的基本用語。（詳見P82）

【例 如】

▶ Wait a moment, please.
　請稍等！

▶ Would you please hold on a second?
　能請你稍等一下嗎？

若是代接電話，不論是要轉接電話或記下電話留言，當需要知道來電者的身份時，則可以婉轉有禮地詢問對方的姓名。（詳見P94）

【例 如】

▶ May I know who is on the line?
　請問你的大名？

▶ Who is this, please?
　請問你是哪一位？

三、結束電話的禮儀

當你要結束通話時，當然少不了要和對方道別，基本的用法就是 "Good-bye"。在說 "Good-bye" 之前，你可以有許多暗示性的說法以提醒對方你想要結束這通電話了（詳見P220）。

【例　如】

▶ It's nice talking to you.
　很高興和你通電話。

▶ I got to go now.
　我要掛斷電話了！

　　當你表達了以上的暗示性語句後，等對方說 "Sure" 或 "OK" 後，就可以直接表達道別（Good-bye）了！

也需要知道的英文知識

　　晚上剛接通電話時的「道晚安」是用 "Good evening"，若是屬於道別性質的道晚安，則要用 "Good night"。

Chapter 3

電話禮儀—聲調清楚

　　「電話溝通」是一種藉由聲音和語言與對方進行溝通的工具，接、打電話時所傳達的語氣、語詞，往往是在「電話溝通」的人際往來的互動間，奠定印象分數的第一個重要關卡。

○ 自信的語調

　　電話溝通，最切忌的就是語調不清楚。你也許會因為要說英文的關係，所以沒有自信，或是聲量過於小而顯得支支吾吾甚至語焉不詳，這些令人不舒服的聲調，聽在電話另一端的人耳裡，都是很不舒服的感覺。之所以會有以上的狀況，都是因為沒有自信說英文的關係。但是換個角度想一想，如果你今天遇到一位外國朋友努力的要用中文和你溝通，你會恥笑對方說得不好嗎？你應該會為對方的用心喝采吧！相同的，外國朋友很輕易就能從你的語調發現英文不是你的母語，你大可大大方方地用最自然的語調和對方溝通。

○ 坦然面對英文不流利的窘境

　　若是你真的說了一口破英文，也沒關係，告訴對

方你的英文真的不太好，請對方見諒，讓對方也能夠
感受到你努力溝通的誠意。

【例　如】

▶ Sorry, I can't speak English very well.
抱歉，我的英文不太好。

○ 請來電者協助

若是實在聽不懂對方所說的話、對方說太快時，
不妨請對方說慢一點或是再說一遍。（詳見180）

【例　如】

▶ Would you speak louder?
能請你說大聲一點嗎？

▶ Pardon?
請再說一遍。

也需要知道的英文知識

"pardon" 的全文是 "I beg your pardon"，
是因為聽不清楚而請對方再說一遍的意思。

Chapter 4

電話禮儀—基本禮貌

很多人容易忽略通電話時的基本禮儀，往往是犯了一些禁忌卻又渾然不覺，以下是一些要注意的基本禮貌，千萬不要因為不當的通電話習慣而壞了自己的人際關係。

（一）愉悅的聲調：

接電話可不是隨隨便便的說聲Hello就可以了，當電話接通後，在對方還沒有發出聲音前，你必須要用"Hello"打招呼，這個第一聲"Hello"也就是中文的「喂」，應該傳達出一種主動、積極、愉快的心情態度。

（二）不可分心翻閱資料：

接聽電話時，切記不要同時間打字、翻閱文件或紙張（除非這通電話有特殊需要），否則會讓對方認為你不專心講電話。

（三）適當搗住話筒：

當你不得不打噴嚏或咳嗽時，請趕緊說一聲"Excuse me"，也請搗住嘴把或話筒，這種噴嚏或是咳嗽聲在另一端聽起來，可是相當不禮貌的。

（四）停止背景音樂：

當你通電話，請禁止一切外界聲音的干擾，像是電視聲、音響聲、廣播聲等，接電話前請先關掉這些聲響。

（五）撥錯電話要先道歉：

若是撥錯電話時，請不要直接掛斷電話，請養成好習慣，先向對方道歉吧！然後向對方確認自己所撥的電話號碼，以免自己又撥錯相同的號碼。（詳見 P187）

【例 如】

▶ Is this 86473663?
這個電話號碼是 86473663 嗎？

▶ Sorry, I must dial the wrong number.
抱歉，我一定是撥錯電話號碼了。

此外，若是接電話前，你的嘴裡有食物、正在喝飲料、嚼口香糖，都請立即停止，因為對方可是會從這些怪異的聲調中發現你的嘴裡「正在忙」，這可是非常不禮貌的行為。

Chapter 5

電話禮儀—
接電話的時機與禮儀

你是不是也有這樣的經驗，打電話給某人時，電話聲響了半天都沒有人來應接，這時你的心情是不是會因此而感到不耐、急躁、困惑等，這些負面的情緒很容易在等不到對方應接電話的同時產生。

○ 三聲內接起電話

不要小看「接電話的時機」，一般來說，電話聲響起三聲內，就必須要應接（answer）電話，尤其在公司裡，來電者有可能是客戶（clients），若是放任電話鈴聲超過太久的次數，難免會讓人有一種不夠積極的觀感，因此三聲之內最好能快速的接起電話。

○ 表明接電話者的身份或單位

此外，當接起電話的時候，最好能夠馬上讓來電者知道所接通的單位為何。你有兩種應接語句可以讓來電者知道你的身份：

一、表明身份

接起電話時，表達了最基本的寒暄 Hi、Hello 之後，你可以用最簡短的語句說明自己的身份，可以是

名字或全名都是可以的。不論是在公司或家裡接的電話，直接表明身份都是適合的。（詳見P77）

【例 如】

► Hello, this is John.
  你好，我是約翰。

► Hello, this is John Smith.
  你好，我是約翰・史密斯。

► Hello. Good morning, John here.
  哈囉，早安！我是約翰。

還要說明的是，若你就是對方來電要找的人時，也可以直接表明「我就是本人」的身份。（詳見P85）

【例 如】

► This is he.
  我就是。（適用在男性受話方）

► This is she.
  我就是。（適用在女性受話方）

二、表明所屬的部門或單位

若你的職位是屬於主管的秘書，那麼你就需要表明這是主管的辦公室。

【例 如】

► John Smith's office.
  （這是）約翰・史密斯的辦公室。

> ▶ This is President Brown's office.
>   這是布朗總裁的辦公室。

> ▶ This is Mr. White's office. May I help you?
>   這是懷特先生的辦公室。可以為你服務嗎？

三、表明公司

　　除了個人的身份之外，也可以利用在接起電話時，直接就表明公司的名稱。

【例 如】

> ▶ Good morning. China Airlines.
>   早安，（這是）中華航空。

> ▶ You've reached the John Smith Corporation.
>   這是約翰史密斯公司。

> ▶ Hello, this is the operator for IBM.
>   您好，這是IBM公司總機。

　　此外，若是在家裡接的電話，則只要接起電話後簡單説Hi、Hello就可以了，此時通常是需要來電者表明他/她的身份。

　　值得一提的是，若對方沒有在接起電話表明身份時，也切忌使用下列的語句："What?"，因為這些語句是屬於會讓聽者覺得不舒服的不禮貌問句。

Chapter 6
電話禮儀—
接電話前就要準備好紙筆

你是不是也有這樣的經驗，匆匆忙忙接了電話後，來電者想要留言（leave a message），你卻找不到紙筆可以寫下留言（take a message）？記住，這種因為你要找紙筆而使來電者等太久的舉動，已經在電話溝通的過程中產生負面的影響。特別是在工作場合中，這可是一大忌諱。

建議不論在家裡或是公司等工作場合，在電話旁邊就要準備好紙筆，如果對方要求留言時，你甚至不用請對方稍等，就可以直接記下對方的留言。這種快速的電話留言反應，將能夠為你贏得不小的掌聲。

此外，若是不得不請對方稍等讓你能夠找紙筆時，也請告訴對方讓你可以拿紙筆記下留言，並輕輕地放下話筒，因為太過於用力放下話筒所產生的聲響，聽在電話另一端的人耳裡，可是一件不好受的噪音。

【例　如】
▶ Please wait. I have to get a piece of paper.
　請稍等，讓我拿一張紙。

▶ Just a minute. I have to get a pencil.
  請稍等，讓我拿一枝筆。

▶ Excuse me. Let me get my pen.
  抱歉，讓我拿我的筆。

　　請對方稍等最好的對待方式還有「按下電話的保留鍵」，讓對方聽一聽音樂，總比讓對方聽見在你的環境中可能發生任何的背景聲音都來得好。

Chapter 7
電話禮儀—打電話的時機

　　到底該什麼時候打電話是最佳的時機呢 (timing)？若是在錯誤的時機打電話給對方，反而會造成對方的困擾，如此一來，不但破壞彼此的關係，更讓對方留下不好的印象。

　　打電話的最佳時機可分為兩的部分來說明：

一、工作場合的電話

　　若是屬於在上班時間與工作有關的電話，建議最佳的去電時機有兩個時段：

　　（一）早上 10 點鐘到 11 點鐘之間。不建議在 9 點鐘一上班就撥電話給對方，是因為若對方還沒有進公司，豈不是讓對方晚到的行徑在對方的公司引起注意。而對方若是准時上班，則有可能還在處理昨天未完成的工作，或是對方還沒有準備好要馬上處理公事，此時撥打電話過去是比較沒有效率的。

　　而不建議在 11 點鐘之後打電話，則是因為若是重要的事情要談，則有可能耽誤到對方吃午餐的時間，這是不禮貌的行為舉動。

　　（二）下午 2 點鐘到 5 點鐘之間。下午 2 點鐘前，對方可能剛用完餐，才回到座位上不久，有可能頭腦也還不是非常清楚，或是還沒有處理完上午的工作，請讓對方有一點喘息的時間。

而5點鐘之後不要去電，則是避免延誤到對方的下班的時間，或是對方正準備要安排明天待處理（To do list）的工作，此時是不宜打電話去打擾對方的。

以上工作場合的去電時機，是泛指一般的工作事務的聯絡，若是遇上緊急重大的事件，則只要是上班時間都可以去電，沒有這方面去電時機的限制。

二、一般家庭生活的電話

一般說來，家庭電話撥打有幾個時間點可以判斷時機是否適合：用餐的時間、起床的時間、就寢的時間，盡可能避過這三個時間點。若是你不確定對方的作息時間，那麼早上9點鐘之前、晚上10點鐘之後，建議不要去電給對方。

若是你真的必須在一個不切當的時間點打電話給對方，也可以先行道歉自己不得不打這通電話，或問對方自己的來電是否已打擾了對方。（詳見P210）

【例　如】

▶ Sorry to call you so late.
抱歉這麼晚打電話給你。
▶ Sorry to call you so early.
抱歉這麼早打電話給你。

Chapter 8

溝通的技巧—稱呼來電者

　　當撥打電話或接起電話而不知道對方的身份時，為了顧及電話溝通的禮儀，還是得尊稱對方，這時候就可以依照來電者的不同性別來尊稱對方。你有以下幾種方式可以稱呼對方：

一、sir（先生）

二、madam（女士）

○ sir 和 madam 的用法

　　在英文中，該如何利用sir（先生）和madam（女士）應用在英文的電話語句中呢？

一、sir（先生）

　　sir表示對「男性」的尊稱。也就是中文口語中經常使用稱呼男性為「先生」的意思。

【例　如】

▶ May I help you, sir?
先生，有我可以協助的嗎？

▶ Yes, sir?
先生，請說！

▶ May I have your name, sir?
先生，請問你的大名？

二、madam（女士）

madam表示對「女性」的尊稱。表示「夫人」、「太太」、「小姐」的尊稱，適用對象為已成年、不分已婚或未婚，也不知姓氏的女性。

【例　如】

▶ Hello, madam. May I help you?
哈囉，女士。有我可以協助的嗎？

▶ Sorry, madam, John is at work.
抱歉，女士，約翰去上班了！

順帶一提，sir和madam的應用不一定是侷限在不知對方姓氏時使用，在某些已知對方身份的中，也可以直呼對方為sir或madam。要特別注意的是，在sir或madam的使用上，後面不加任何的姓氏或名字。

此外，若是接電話時已知對方的姓氏時，則可以利用對方姓氏的方式尊稱對方：

一、Mr. + 姓氏（某某先生）

二、Mrs. + 姓氏（某某女士）

三、Miss + 姓氏（某某小姐）

○ Mr./ Mrs./ Miss 的用法

在英文中，該如何利用Mr./ Mrs./ Miss應用在英文的電話語句中呢？請看以下的說明：

一、Mr. + 姓氏（某某先生）

Mr.是mister的簡稱，可以適用於男性的姓氏

（family name）、全名（full name）或職務（position）之前。

【例 如】

► Mr. Jones
  瓊斯先生

► Mr. Bill Jones
  比爾·瓊斯先生

► Mr. Chairman
  主席大人

► Good afternoon, Mr. Brown.
  午安，布朗先生。

在這裡要特別注意常犯的一個錯誤用法，Mr.不能使用在名字（name）之前，例如 "Mr. John" 就是一個錯誤的用法。

二、Mrs. + 姓氏（某某女士）

Mrs.是mistress的簡稱，是指對已婚婦女的尊稱，用於已婚女性的夫姓之前，用法和Mr.一樣，也可以適用於姓氏、全名或職務之前。

【例 如】

► Mrs. Taylor
  泰勒太太

► Is this Mrs. Taylor?
  請問是泰勒太太嗎？

► Hello, Mrs. Taylor, how are you today?
  哈囉，泰勒太太，妳今天好嗎？

三、Miss + 姓氏（某某小姐）

是指對未婚女性的尊稱，不論是年輕或年長的女性都適用。用法也和 Mr. 及 Mrs. 一樣，可以適用於姓氏、全名或職務之前。

【例　如】

▶ Miss Green
  格林小姐
▶ Miss Alaska/America
  阿拉斯加/美國小姐（通常是指選美小姐所代表的地區或國家）
▶ Miss Green called you this morning.
  格林小姐今天早上有打電話給你。

此外，Miss 也表示對年輕或年長女性的正式口語稱呼，目的是要引起對方的注意。

【例　如】

▶ Hey, Miss, you dropped a glove!
  嘿，小姐，妳的手套掉在地上了！

也需要知道的英文知識

在英文中有 Mr. Right 的稱呼，指的可不是「Right 先生」，而是指女性的「理想丈夫」人選的意思。也就是理想的另一半（ideal mate）或心靈伴侶（soul mate）的意思。

Chapter 9

溝通的技巧—寒暄

俗話說「禮多人不怪」，當你接起電話時，禮貌性地寒暄問候來電者是絕對必要的，尤其在工作場合，任何一通電話都可能是商務上的重要客戶，千萬不可漏掉這個重要的寒暄問候。（詳見P198）

一、依照時間的寒暄

可以依照你接電話的時間來作為寒暄的依據。像是一大早剛進公司時，就非常適合道早安。

【例 如】

▶ Hello. Good morning.
哈囉，早安！

若是過了早上 11 點鐘之後，因為時間已經接近中午了，則不建議使用 "Good morning" 問候。若是過了下午 1 點鐘之後，則可使用道午安的問候語。

【例 如】

▶ Good afternoon.
午安！

"Good afternoon" 的問候方式，可以一直使用到下午 5 點鐘之前，之後則因為接近晚上的時間，便不再建議使用。

若是在夜間6點鐘之後，則可以説 "Good evening"。

▶ Good evening, Mr. Jones.
　晚安！瓊斯先生。

二、簡潔的的寒暄

最簡潔的寒暄問候則是Hi和Hello。若是覺得這種問候方式顯得過於精簡、單調，也可以順便説出自己的身份或是服務的公司，以增加和對方的親切感。

【例　如】
▶ Hello. This is Nancy.
　哈囉！我是南西。
▶ Hello, I'm Nancy with IBM.
　哈囉！我是IBM公司的南西。

三、說出對方名字的寒暄

根據溝通學專家的研究分析，最能夠和對方套交情的寒暄方式就是不斷的提及對方的名字，因此建議在對方接起電話的同時，就要能夠知道對方的身份，並喊出對方的名字。若是想要讓電話者對你增加印象分數，則可以同時告知對方自己的身份。

【例　如】
▶ Hi, Jack.
　嗨，傑克。
▶ Hello, Jack?
　喂，你是傑克嗎？

▶ Jack, this is David.
　傑克，我是大衛。

▶ Jack, it's me David.
　傑克，我是大衛。

四、好久不見的寒暄

當接電話者是你很久沒有聯絡的對象時，就可以簡單地問候一下對方的近況，讓對方有一種你很關心他的貼心感受。

【例　如】

▶ Long time no see! How have you been?
　好久不見！你好嗎？

Chapter 10
溝通的技巧—自我介紹

電話溝通成功與否的重要前提之一，就是用最短、最快的方式讓對方知道你的身份。（詳見P78）以下有幾種方式可以在電話中快速地表明自己的身份：

一、說明自己的姓名

短暫的Hi或Hello後，直接說出自己的名字，是最簡單的表明身份的方式。可以依照你和對方的熟識程度來表明身份。

【例 如】

▶ Hi, this is Luke.
嗨，我是路克。

▶ Hello, this is Kate White.
哈囉，我是凱特・懷特。

▶ Hi, John, this is David.
嗨，約翰，我是大衛。

▶ Hi, Mr. Smith, this is David Jones.
嗨，史密斯先生，我是大衛・瓊斯。

▶ Good afternoon, this is David Jones speaking.
午安，我是大衛・瓊斯。

但是只是說自己的名字之前，請確定對方對你的
名字是熟悉的，否則對方聽了你的名字後若還是認不
出你，豈不是造成雙方尷尬嗎？

二、說明自己的身份

你的身份可以是同事、商業往來的伙伴、朋友、
同學、親戚等，都是一種提醒對方的作用，說明身份
有助於對方在最短的時間內瞭解你可能的來電目的。

【例　如】

▶ Hello, David, this is Sarah, your cousin.
　哈囉，大衛，我是莎拉，你的表姊妹。

▶ This is John Jones from BBC Corporation.
　我是BBC公司的約翰‧瓊斯。

三、說明自己的職務

通常會說明職務的稱號，代表彼此工作上的關
係，可以是對方平常對你使用的稱呼。若是對方平常
沒有以職位來稱呼你，千萬不要自作聰明加上職稱，
免得徒增對方的困擾。

【例　如】

▶ This is Dr. Jones.
　我是瓊斯醫生。

▶ This is Professor Jones.
　我是瓊斯教授。

Chapter 11
溝通的技巧—去電找人

「電話」是你對外溝通的重要工具之一，如何以成功的電話溝通，來建立公司或個人的最佳形象與效率？從你撥打電話的那一刻開始，每一個流程都佔有舉足輕重的地位。

撥打電話之前，除了要注意前一章節所提「注意打電話的時機」之外，你去電表明要找某人來聽電話的語句，也會決定這是否是一通成功的電話溝通。

撥打電話找受話方來聽電話的方式有很多種，大致可以分為以下幾種表達方式（詳見P69），以下將分別說明，不論是公司場合或是一般家庭生活，都非常適用以下的語句，建議您不妨背誦較順口的一兩句，以應付不時之需。

一、直接說明要找受話方

電話接通後，直接告訴對方自己要找某人講電話。等於是間接地請對方幫自己轉接電話。常用的單字為 speak 和 talk。

【例 如】

▶ I'd like to speak to Mr. Baker.
　我要和貝克先生說話。

▶ I'd like to talk to John.
　我要和約翰說話。

二、詢問是否可以和受話方通話

　　用詢問的語氣，請求和某人通電話，通常是婉轉而客氣的一種語氣。常用的詢問語句為以may開頭的問句。

【例　如】

▶ Hello, may I speak to Mr. Smith?
　喂，我要找史密斯先生說話。

▶ Hi, Judy, may I speak to Kate?
　嗨，茱蒂，我要找凱特說話。

▶ May I speak to Mr. Baker, please?
　請找貝克先生聽電話。

▶ Hello, can I talk to Mrs. Stone?
　哈囉，我要找史東女士說話。

三、請受話方來接電話

　　電話接通後，確認接電話者不是你要找的受話方，直接請對方代為轉接你的來電給受話方。

【例　如】

▶ Can you put Mr. Smith on the phone?
　請史密斯先生來聽電話好嗎？

▶ Could you put me through to David, please?
　請幫我轉接電話給大衛。

▶ Could you transfer me to his line?
可以請你幫我轉接電話給他嗎？

四、詢問受話方是否有空接電話

詢問接電話者，你要找的受話方是否有空可以講電話，此句型在你可能預知受話方正好有事在忙的情境時使用。

【例　如】

▶ Is Mr. Smith available now?
史密斯先生現在有空嗎？

五、詢問受話方是否在

你不確定受話方是否在你所撥電話的地點，因此婉轉地請問接電話者，受話方是否在此處。

【例　如】

▶ Is Mr. Smith there?
史密斯先生在嗎？
▶ Is your manager around?
你們經理在嗎？

六、詢問受話方是否回來了

你預知受話方可能不在，或是你先前已經來電過了，所以詢問接電者受話方是否已經回來了。

49

【例 如】

▶ Has Mr. Smith come back?
史密斯先生回來了嗎?

▶ Is Mr. Smith in yet?
史密斯先生進來了嗎?

　　以上的打電話找受話方的語句雖然未必都是和 speak 或 talk 有關,但是都足以表達你要找受話方來聽電話的意思。

Chapter 12
溝通的技巧—請對方稍候

　　電話禮儀是存在於每一段通話的小細節中,任何一段小細節的禮儀都不能忽略,否則電話溝通過程就容易出現瑕疵,影響的結果會有多大?往往是很難評估的。更甚者也許會導致雙方人際間的誤解或誤會。

　　本章節要説明的是「請對方稍候」的電話用語。在電話溝通的過程中,需要請對方稍候的情況有兩種:

　　一、幫來電者轉接電話

　　二、臨時有事,必須短暫地暫停通話

　　在你請對方稍候不要掛斷電話時,一定要謹記,先告訴對方你很抱歉(Excuse me),再説明你必須請對方稍候的要求。(詳見P101)

○ 請對方稍候不要掛斷電話

一、幫來電者轉接電話

　　當你接起電話,發現來電者要找的人不是你而是其他人時,你就有義務幫來電者轉接電話。轉接電話前,你就必須告知對方稍候不要掛斷電話。

【例　如】

▶ Hold on a second.
　請稍等!

▶ Please hold for a moment, Mr. Baker.
請稍等,貝克先生!

▶ Hold on for a while please.
請稍候!

▶ Could I put you on hold for a second?
能否請你稍待片刻?

▶ I'll transfer your call now. Hold on.
我現在幫你轉接電話!不要掛斷!

二、臨時有事,必須暫停通話

　　若是正在和對方通話時,正好臨時有事必須請對方稍待片刻時,就可以請對方稍等不要掛斷電話(Don't hang up),自己馬上就回來。

【例 如】

▶ Wait a moment, please. I'll be back with you.
請稍候!我馬上回來。

▶ Hang on a second.
等一下不要掛斷電話!

▶ Could you hang on a second? I've got a call on line 1.
你可以等一下嗎?我有一通待接電話在一線。

▶ Don't hang up.
不要掛斷電話!

　　值得一提的是,當你請對方稍候,並重新回來接電話後,也可以告訴對方你回來聽電話了。

【例 如】

▶ I'm back.
　我回來了！

▶ Where was I?
　我說到哪？

▶ Are you still there?
　你還在線上嗎？

▶ Thank you for waiting.
　謝謝等久了！

　　若是讓對方等了很長一段時間，記得要先致歉讓對方等太久喔！

【例 如】

▶ Sorry to keep you waiting.
　抱歉讓你久等了！

▶ I'm sorry to have kept you waiting.
　抱歉讓你久等了！

Chapter 13
溝通的技巧—
詢問對方的身份

　　若是你接到一通電話時（不論是不是找你的電話，或是只是幫其他人代接的電話），對方並沒有主動告知他的身份（也許對方疏忽了），而你也認不出對方的身份時，你就應該主動請對方表明自己的身份（詳見P94）。有以下幾種方式可以得知對方的身份：

一、請對方直接表明姓名

　　假使你認不出對方的聲音甚至不太確定對方就是你認識的某人，就必須請對方明白告知他的名字，千萬不要用猜測的方式得知對方的身份，免得猜錯對方的身份反而讓彼此都很尷尬。

【例　如】

▶ Who is this?
　你是哪一位？

▶ May I have your name, please?
　請問你的大名？

▶ May I have your last name, please?
　請問你貴姓？

在上述問句中，要特別注意第一句 "Who is this?"，是屬於慣用法，this 不可以用其他主詞替代。

二、禮貌性地詢問對方的身份

當你在工作場合接到一通電話，也許你認不出對方的身份，也或許你要幫同事轉接電話，都可以禮貌而隱喻性地詢問對方的身份。

【例 如】

▶ May I know who is calling?
請問你的大名？

▶ May I ask who is calling?
請問你是哪一位？

▶ May I know who is speaking?
我能知道你的名字嗎？

三、婉轉地請對方告知身份

除了上述兩種詢問對方身份的問句之外，還可以用「要轉接電話」為由，請對方告知身份。

【例 如】

▶ May I tell her who is calling?
需要我告訴她是誰來電嗎？

▶ May I tell him who is calling?
需要我告訴他是誰來電嗎？

Chapter 14

溝通的技巧─轉接電話

　　當你接到一通必須要轉接的電話時，除了告訴對方「稍候」（wait a moment）之外，也可以直接告訴來電者你會幫他轉這通電話。讓對方能更放心的等待電話轉接，也會對你的協助產生好感（詳見P114）。轉接電話的說法有以下幾種方式：

一、告知會轉接電話

　　最基本也最簡單的表達方式，是讓對方知道自己準備要轉接他/她的電話。

【例　如】

▶ I'll put you through.
　我幫你接過去。

▶ I'll connect you.
　我幫你轉接電話。

二、會立即轉接電話

　　為了不讓對方產生久候的疑慮，告知對方會馬上轉接這通電話。

【例　如】

▶ I'll transfer your call right away.
　我馬上轉接你的電話。

三、轉接電話給某人

再次和對方確認，你將會把此通電話轉接給某位特定的受話方。

【例　如】

▶ OK, Mr. Jones, I'll put you through to John.
好的，瓊斯先生，我來幫你轉接電話給約翰。

四、告知會請某人來接電話

告知來電者，自己將會請受話方來聽電話。這句話是特別強調「請受話方來接電話」的用語。

【例　如】

▶ I'll get John to the phone.
我請約翰來接電話。

五、轉接電話到相關部門

若對方要通話的對象是某部門，也應該要告訴對方自己會將電話轉接給相關部門。

【例　如】

▶ I'll transfer you to the sales department.
我會把你的電話轉到行銷售部門。

Chapter 15

溝通的技巧—電話留言

當你幫某人接電話或是因為受話方不在而無法接聽電話時，身為接聽電話者，你有義務代為記下電話留言。（詳見P145）

一、是否要留下留言

詢問來電者是否願意留言，因為來電者也許不願意留言，所以可以先詢問對方是否有任何留言要代為傳達。

【例　如】

▶ Would you like to leave a message?
  你要留下留言嗎？

二、代為記下留言

告知來電者，自己願意幫受話方記下留言。

【例　如】

▶ May I take a message?
  需要我(替你)留言嗎？

▶ Shall I take a message?
  我可以(替你)留言嗎？

三、記下留言並代為轉達

告訴來電者，你非常樂意幫他記下留言給受話方，並且保證會轉達留言。

【例　如】

▶ May I take your name and number and have him call you back?
　請問你的大名，我會請他回電給你。

四、有留言請對方傳達

當你去電時，受話方不在或無法接電話時，你就可以要求接電話者代為轉達留言。你應該禮貌性詢問對方自己是否可以留下電話留言。（詳見P158）

【例　如】

▶ May I leave a message?
　我可以留言嗎？
▶ I'd like to leave a message.
　我要留言。

若是某人來電請你代為解決問題，而你無法回答或不想回答時，也可以幫來電者轉接電話給可以幫忙解決問題的人。

【例　如】

▶ I'm sorry I don't know but I'd be happy to pass the message on to John.
　抱歉，我不知道，但是我很樂意幫你把訊息轉達給約翰。

　　若來電者留下電話留言，請務必確認你有記下對方的姓名、電話號碼、來電的時間及相關的其他電話留言。並記得將留言轉給受話方。

　　此外，受話方很容易就忽略留言甚至是沒有注意到你的留言，建議固定一處是專門在記留言的地方，像是家裡，可以選擇在電話旁的留言本，或是將留言貼在冰箱上。若是在公司的場合，則可以準備一個留言板或是在受話方桌面的一個固定點放置留言。

也需要知道的英文知識

(一)你知道以下數字的英文怎麼念嗎？

0	zero	5	five
1	one	6	six
2	two	7	seven
3	three	8	eight
4	four	9	nine

(二) 你知道以下電話的念法嗎？

Q 8647-3663

A eight-six-four-seven-three-six-six-three

Q 2649-1037

A two-six-four-nine-one-oh-three-seven

〔註〕當一群數字的時候，0可以念做 "oh"

Chapter 16

溝通的技巧—回電

當你希望對方回你電話時，應該要怎麼說呢？最常用的片語就是 "call back"。在何種情況下需要請對方回電呢？也許是你臨時有事，不能再繼續和對方通話，也許是你留言希望對方回你電話等。（詳見P168）

一、一般性要求回/來電

適用於一般非緊急事件的情境，提醒對方之後要再保持聯絡，所以要回電給你。

【例　如】

▶ Call me back, OK?
　回電話給我好嗎？

▶ Please ask her to call me back.
　請她回我電話。

▶ Call me again any time.
　歡迎隨時再打電話過來。

▶ Call again when you've got time.
　你有空的話可以打電話給我。

二、詢問是否會回電

利用詢問的語氣，請求對方再來電。

【例 如】

▶ Would you mind calling again later?
　你可以晚一點再回電嗎？

▶ Would you mind calling back around three?
　你可以大概三點鐘再回電嗎？

三、強烈地要求回電

　　通常會強烈地要求對方務必回你電話的情況是屬於比較重要、緊急的事件。你可以在留下請對方回你電話的要求語句中，順帶說明希望受話方回電的時間。

【例 如】

▶ Tell her to call me back as soon as possible.
　告訴她盡快回我電話。

▶ Get him to call me back tomorrow.
　叫他明天回我電話。

▶ Would you have him call me back at ten?
　能請他十點鐘的時候回我電話嗎？

▶ You'll call me back, won't you?
　你會回我電話吧，對嗎？

Chapter 17

溝通的技巧─再來電

　　電話溝通的好處就是，只要有電話號碼，你隨時都可以找得到對方（當然還是要注意打電話的時機）。當受話方不在（也許是因為短暫外出、剛離開座位），或是正在忙無法接聽電話，你就必須要等一陣子再打電話過去。

一、告知對方會再來電

　　告訴對方，自己晚一點會再打電話過來，沒有特定再來電的時間說明。

【例　如】

▶ I'll call back later.
　我待會再打電話過來。

▶ I'll try again later.
　我稍後會再試著打電話過來。

二、會再來電的時間

　　先預估自己會再來電的時間，也許是幾分鐘之後，也可以在某個特定的時間或日期。

【例　如】

▶ I'll call back in 5 minutes.
　我五分鐘後會再打電話過來。

► I'll call back in an hour.
　我一個小時後會再打電話過來。
► I'll call back at four o'clock.
　我四點鐘會再打電話過來。
► I'll call back tomorrow.
　我明天會再打電話過來。

三、詢問何時可以再回電

　　當你想要再回電，卻不知哪個時間比較適合時，就可以問對方你什麼時間再來電會比較方便。

【例　如】
► When should I call back then?
　那我應該什麼時候回電？

四、請對方稍後再來電

　　婉轉地建議對方可以稍後再打電話過來，通常適用在受話方忙時不在、正在忙無法接電話等情境中，或是你現在無法替對方解決問題，希望對方給你一段時間時，也可以請對方晚一點再打電話過來。

【例　如】
► Maybe you can call back later.
　也許你可以晚一點再打電話過來。
► Why don't you just call back later?
　你何不晚一點再撥電話過來。
► Could you call again after three?
　你可以三點鐘之後再來電嗎？

Chapter 18

溝通的技巧—聽不清楚/ 請對方再說一遍

　　電話溝通的過程可能會發生的意外不甚枚舉，當發生一些不可預期的事情時，大可以大大方方地請對方協助你。千萬不要因為不好意思而假裝自己理解對方的陳述，若是屆時被對方識破，反而得不償失。匯整電話溝通過程中，可能發生的狀況：

一、線路不良

　　不良的線路可是會讓電話溝通的效果打折扣，萬一發生線路不良的情況，就直接告訴對方線路不好，再決定是否要重撥電話或稍後再聯絡。（詳見P181）

【例　如】

▶ Something's wrong with this phone.
電話線路有點問題。

二、要接插撥電話

　　萬一你正在等的一通電話正好打進來，而你碰巧也還在電話中時，不妨告訴對方你必須要先接另一通重要的電話。

【例 如】

▶ I'm afraid I have a call on another line.
抱歉我要接插撥電話。

三、請對方調整說話速度或音量

因為英文不是你熟悉的語言，若是對方說話速度太快甚至音量不夠大時，很容易造成誤解，可以告訴對方配合你的聽力，說話時的速度稍做修正。

【例 如】

▶ Would you slow down a little, please?
可以請你說慢一點嗎？

▶ You're talking too fast. I can't keep up.
你說太快，我跟不上。

▶ Could you speak a little louder?
你可以說大聲一點嗎？

四、不懂對方的意思

電話溝通最忌諱不懂裝懂，若是對方的言論造成你的理解困擾，請直接告訴對方你不懂他的意思。

【例 如】

▶ I don't understand what you just said.
我不懂你剛剛說什麼。

▶ What did you say just now?
你剛剛說什麼？

五、請對方再說一次

因為線路品質不良、說話太快或音量太小等問題，可以請對方再說一遍。

【例 如】

▶ I beg your pardon?
你說什麼？

▶ Could you say that again, please?
你可以再說一遍嗎？

Chapter 1

打電話

【 Unit 01 】致電給特定受話方

> # Can I talk to Sarah, please?
> 我能和莎拉說話嗎?

實用會話

A Good morning.
早安。

B Good morning. Can I talk to Sarah, please?
早安。我能和莎拉說話嗎?

A Hold on, please.
請稍等。

B Thank you.
謝謝你。

(稍後)

A Sorry, but she's out.
抱歉,她出去了。

B Would you tell her Raymond called, please?
能請你告訴她雷蒙打過電話嗎?

相關用語

► Hello, may I speak to John, please?
哈囉,我能和約翰說話嗎?

► Is your manager around?
你們經理在嗎?

關鍵單字

► hold on 不要掛斷電話

【 Unit 02 】打電話找人

Is John around?
約翰在嗎?

實用會話

A
Is John around?
約翰在嗎?

B
I'm sorry, but he just went out.
很抱歉,他剛出去。

B
Do you know when he would come back?
你知道他什麼時候會回來嗎?

B
I have no idea. Would you like to leave a message?
我不知道。你要留言嗎?

A
Sure, my number is 86473663.
好的,我的號碼是86473663。

B
I'll have him call you back.
我會請他回你電話。

相關用語

▶Is Sarah there, please?

請問莎拉在嗎?

關鍵單字

▶ around 在附近

▶ leave 留下、留置

▶ call someone back 回電話給(某人)

【Unit 03】打電話給不特定的人

Could I talk to Carrie or Sunny?
我能和凱莉或桑尼說話嗎？

實用會話

A
Is Maria in?
瑪麗亞在嗎？

B
Maria is not in right now.
瑪麗亞現在不在。

A
Could I talk to Carrie or Sunny?
那我可以找凱莉或是桑尼說話嗎？

B
Carrie is out to lunch and Sunny is not at his desk.
凱莉去吃午餐了，而桑尼不在他的位子上。

A
Could I leave the three of them a message?
我能留話給他們三個人嗎？

B
Of course. Let me get a pencil.
當然可以。讓我拿支筆。

關鍵單字

▶ get　拿、取(某物)
▶ pencil　筆、鉛筆

【Unit 04】詢問受話方今天是否在

Is Sarah in today?
莎拉今天在嗎？

實用會話

A	Is Sarah in today?
	莎拉今天在嗎？
B	No, she's out of town.
	不，她出城去了。
A	When will she come back?
	她什麼時候會回來？
B	She'll be back next Friday.
	她下星期五才會回來。
A	I couldn't wait for such a long time.
	我不能等那麼久！
B	Maybe you could call her cell phone.
	或許你可以打電話到她的手機。

相關用語

►Is she here yet?

她進來了嗎？

關鍵單字

►next 下一個、下一次
►a long time 一段長時間
►cell phone 手機、行動電話

【Unit 05】詢問受話方是否回來了

Is Sarah in yet?
莎拉回來了嗎？

實用會話

A Is Sarah in yet?
莎拉回來了嗎？

B Yes, but she just stepped away.
是的，但是她剛剛又暫時走開了。

A Well...hmm....
嗯…這個嘛…

B Would you care to leave a message?
你要留言嗎？

A Sure, my number is...
好的，我的號碼是…

B Hold on a second. She just came back. I'll put you through.
等一下，她剛好回來了。我幫你轉接過去。

關鍵單字

▶ step away　暫時離開
▶ care to　想要做(某事)、從事(某事)
▶ put someone through　幫(某人)轉接(電話)

【Unit 06】確認受話方的身份

Is this Mrs. White?
你是懷特太太嗎？

實用會話

A Hello?
喂？

B Is this Mrs. White?
是懷特太太嗎？

A No, this is her secretary.
不，我是她的秘書。

B Sorry. May I speak to Mrs. White?
抱歉！我能和懷特太太說話嗎？

A Wait a moment, please.
請稍等。

B Thank you.
謝謝你。

相關用語

► Hi, is this David?

嗨，你是大衛嗎？

► David?

是大衛嗎？

關鍵單字

► secretary　秘書

【Unit 07】確認所打的電話號碼

Is this 86473663?

這個電話號碼是 **86473663** 嗎?

實用會話

A
Hello?
喂?

B
Hello, is John there?
哈囉,約翰在嗎?

A
I'm sorry, you have the wrong number.
抱歉,你打錯電話號碼囉!

B
Oh...is this 86473663?
喔…這是86473663嗎?

A
No, it's not. You have the wrong number.
不,不是!你打錯電話號碼了!

B
I'm sorry.
抱歉!

A
That's OK.
沒關係!

【Unit 08】去電表明身份，並告知找某人

This is Luke calling for Sarah.
我是路克，打電話來要找莎拉。

實用會話

A
Modern Beauty Salon, may I help you?
摩登美容沙龍，可以為你服務嗎？

B
Good afternoon. This is Luke calling for Sarah.
午安，我是路克，打電話來找莎拉。

A
Would you wait a moment, please?
請稍等。

B
Thank you.
謝謝你。

(電話轉接中)

C
This is Sarah.
我是莎拉。

B
Hi, Sarah. This is Luke calling...
嗨，莎拉，我是路克…

相關用語

▶Hi, this is Luke.

嗨，我是路克。

關鍵單字

▶ salon 沙龍美容中心

▶ calling for 打電話給(某人)

【Unit 09】打招呼後，表明身份

Hi, Jennifer. This is David.
嗨，珍妮佛。我是大衛。

實用會話

A
Hello?
喂？

B
Hello, is Jennifer there?
哈囉，珍妮佛在嗎？

A
This is Jennifer.
我就是！

B
Hi, Jennifer. This is David.
嗨，珍妮佛。我是大衛。

A
David?
大衛？

B
David Baker.
我是大衛‧貝克。

A
Oh, David. Hi, how are you?
喔，大衛喔！嗨，你好嗎？

B
Good, thanks.
不錯，謝謝關心！

相關用語

►Hello, David, this is Sarah, your cousin.
哈囉，大衛，我是莎拉，你的表姊妹。

【Unit 10】告知不用留言，會再回電

No, I'll call back later.
不用！我等會會再打電話過來！

實用會話

A May I speak to John or David, please?
我可以和約翰或大衛説話嗎？

B I'm sorry, but they aren't here right now.
Who is calling, please?
抱歉，他們現在不在。請問你的大名？

A Kate Jones.
我是凱特‧瓊斯。

B May I take a message, Miss Jones?
瓊斯小姐，需要我記下留言嗎？

A No, I'll call back later.
不用！我等會會再打電話過來！

相關用語

▶I'll try to call back later.
我會試著晚一點再打電話過來！

【Unit 11】請代為轉告有來電

> # Just tell him I called.
> 告訴他我有來電就好！

實用會話

A Good morning. May I help you?
早安！可以為你服務嗎？

B Yes. May I speak to Mr. Baker, please? This is David Jones.
是的。我可以和貝克先生説話嗎？我是大衛・瓊斯。

A Sorry, Mr. Jones. Mr. Baker isn't here right now. Would you like to leave a message?
抱歉，瓊斯先生。貝克先生現在不在。你要留言嗎？

B Well, no. Just tell him I called.
喔，不用了！告訴他我有來電就好！

A OK, Mr. Jones.
好的，瓊斯先生。

相關用語

▶ Would you tell him that Charlie called?
可以請你告訴他查理有打電話來嗎？

【Unit 12】詢問對方昨晚是否有來電

> ### Did you call me last night?
> 你昨天晚上有打電話給我嗎？

實用會話

A | This is John Jones.　Is David there?
　　我是約翰‧瓊斯。大衛在嗎？

B | OK, Mr. Jones, I'll put you through to him.
　　好的，瓊斯先生，我來幫你轉接電話給他。

　　（電話轉接中）

C | Hi, John.　What can I do for you?
　　嗨，約翰。有什麼需要我為你效勞嗎？

A | Did you call me last night?
　　你昨天晚上有打電話給我嗎？

B | No.　Why?
　　沒有啊！怎麼了？

關鍵單字

▶ answer　接電話

Chapter 2

接起電話

【 Unit 01 】電話剛撥通時

> # Hello?
> 喂？

實用會話

A	Hello? 喂？
B	May I speak to Dr. Brown? 我能和布朗教授說話嗎？
A	May I know who is calling? 請問你的大名？
B	This is Jason Baker. 我是傑生·貝克。
A	Wait a moment, please. I'll get him. 請稍等，我去叫他來（接電話）。
B	Thank you. 謝謝你。

關鍵單字

▶ speak 說話、談話、交談、講起
▶ wait 等待、盼望、期待、期望

【Unit 02】接起電話時的禮貌詢問

> # May I help you?
>
> 可以為你服務嗎？

實用會話

A Norman Publisher. May I help you?
諾曼出版社。可以為你服務嗎？

B Hello, may I speak to John, please?
哈囉，我能和約翰説話嗎？

A Just a minute, please.
請等一下。

B OK.
好的。

（稍後）

A I'm sorry, but he's not at his desk now.
很抱歉，他現在不在座位上。

B Could I leave him a message?
我能留言給他嗎？

A Sure. Wait a moment, please.
好的！請稍候！

關鍵單字

▶ publisher　出版者、發行者、出版社
▶ at someone's desk(某人)在位子上、在座位前

【Unit 03】我就是你要找的人

> # This is he.
>
> 我就是本人。

實用會話

A
Hello, can I talk to John, please?
哈囉，我能和約翰説話嗎？

B
This is he.
我就是本人。(適用男性本人接電話)

A
Hi, I am Jack, the salesman of the Stars Company.
嗨，我是傑克，星光公司的銷售員。

B
What can I do for you, Jack?
傑克，有什麼需要我為你效勞嗎？

A
Do you have a minute now? I want to talk to you about our new products.
你現在有空嗎？我要和你談一談有關我們新產品的事。

B
Sure. Keep going.
好的！説吧！

相關用語

▶This is she.

我就是本人。（適用女性本人接電話）

▶Speaking.

我就是本人，請説！

▶Hello, John speaking.

　哈囉！我就是約翰本人，請說。

▶This is Dr. Chang. What can I do for you?

　我是張博士。有什麼需要我為你效勞嗎？

【Unit 04】接起電話直接表明身份

> ### This is Dr. Ford.
> 我就是福特教授。

實用會話

A Is Dr. Ford there?
福特教授在嗎？

B This is Dr. Ford.
我就是福特教授。

A Hi, I'm Jack's father. I want to talk about Jack's behavior in school.
嗨，我是傑克的父親，我向要談一談傑克在學校的行為。

B Hi, Mr. Gates, I was just about to call you.
嗨，蓋茲先生，我剛好要打電話給你。

A I'm really sorry about what Jack had done in school.
我很抱歉傑克在學校所作的事。

B That's nothing. What I really care about is what he said.
那沒關係。我真正在意的是他說過的話。

相關用語

▶Hello, good morning, John here.

哈囉，早安！我是約翰！

關鍵單字

▶ nothing　無關緊要的、微不足道的

【 Unit 05 】我就是本人，請說！

Speaking.
我就是本人，請說！

實用會話

A Hello, may I speak to Mr. Smith?
喂，我要找史密斯先生。

B Speaking.
我就是本人，請說！

A Hi, Mr. Smith, this is David Jones.
嗨，史密斯先生，我是大衛・瓊斯。

B Yes, Mr. Jones, what can I do for you?
是的，瓊斯先生，有什麼需要我為你效勞嗎？

A I'm calling to see if your house is still for sale.
我是打電話來問你的房子是否還在出售中。

相關用語

▶ This is John speaking.
我就是約翰本人，請說。

【Unit 06】本人接起電話並確認身份

> ### Yes, speaking.
> 是的，請説！

實用會話

A Hello, is this David?
哈囉，是大衛嗎？

B Yes, speaking.
是的，請説！

A Hi, David, this is Sarah, your neighbor.
嗨，大衛，我是莎拉，你的鄰居。

B Sarah? Oh, Sarah, of course. How are you doing?
莎拉？喔！是莎拉喔！你好嗎？

A I'm OK. Thank you. Look, I really need your help.
還不錯！謝謝關心！是這樣的，我真的需要你的幫忙！

B What happened?
怎麼啦？

【Unit 07】和來電者通話的就是受話方本人

You are talking to him.

我就是本人。

實用會話

A
Hello?

哈囉？

B
Hello, may I talk to Dr. Block, please?

哈囉，我能和布拉克教授說話嗎？

A
You are talking to him.

你正和他說話。(適用男性本人接電話)

B
Hi, Dr. Block, I'm Jeffery. I'd like to make an appointment with you.

嗨，布拉克教授，我是傑佛瑞，我想要和你約個時間見面。

A
Hi, Jeffery. Let me see my schedule. When do you prefer?

嗨，傑佛瑞。我看看我的行程。你想要什麼時候？

B
How about ten o'clock tomorrow morning?

明天早上十點鐘如何？

相關用語

►You are talking to her.

我就是本人。(適用女性本人接電話)

關鍵單字

►appointment 約定、預約、約會

【Unit 08】受話方接起轉接電話時

John here.
我是約翰。

實用會話

A You've reached Mr. Smith's office. How may I help you?
這是史密斯先生的辦公室。有什麼需要我協助嗎？

B Yes, I'd like to talk to John.
是的，我要和約翰說話。

A Wait a moment, please. I'll transfer your call.
請稍等。我幫你轉接電話。

B Thank you.
謝謝你。

(電話轉接中)

C John here.
我是約翰。

B Hi, John. This is Jack.
嗨，約翰！我是傑克。

相關用語

▶This is John.
我是約翰。

關鍵單字

▶transfer　轉接(電話等)

【Unit 09】寒暄並表明身份

Good morning, this is Joe speaking.
早安，我是喬伊。

實用會話

A Good morning, this is Joe speaking.
早安，我是喬伊。

B Hi, I'm looking for the manager of sales.
嗨，我要找銷售經理。

A This is he. What can I do for you?
我就是。有什麼需要我為你效勞嗎？

B Hi, Mr. Smith, I had some problem with my orders. I was wondering if you could help me out.
嗨，史密斯先生，我對我的訂單有一些問題。我在想你是否可以幫我解決！

B Sure, sir. May I have your last name, please?
好的，先生！請問你貴姓？

A Baker. Joe Baker.
貝克。我是喬伊‧貝克。

B Please hold for a moment, Mr. Baker.
請稍候，貝克先生！

【Unit 10】隨口問來電者有何事

> # Yes?
> 有什麼事？

實用會話

A　May I talk to Tad?
　　我能和陶德說話嗎？

B　Speaking.
　　請說。

A　This is Jason Jones calling from EC Company.
　　我是EC公司的傑森‧瓊斯。

B　Yes?
　　有什麼事？

A　I'm the manager of the marketing department.
　　我是行銷部門的經理。

B　Hi, Mr. Jones, are you going to explain the new plans to me?
　　嗨，瓊斯先生你要向我解釋新的計劃嗎？

關鍵單字

▶ marketing　行銷、銷售
▶ explain　說明、解釋、澄清、辨明

Chapter 3

確認來電者身份

【Unit 01】禮貌性確認來電者身份

> # May I ask who is calling?
> 請問你是哪位？

實用會話

A Hello, is Peter there?
哈囉，彼得在嗎？

B Hold on, please.
請稍等。

A Sure.
好的。

（稍後）

B He's in the shower right now. May I ask who is calling?
他現正在淋浴。請問你是哪位？

A This is Ellen, his boss. I'll call back later. Thank you.
我是艾倫，他的老闆。我待會再打電話來。謝謝你。

B You are welcome. Bye.
不客氣，再見。

相關用語

▶May I know who is calling?
可以告訴我你的大名嗎？

▶May I have your name, please?
請問你的大名？

【Unit 02】詢問線上是哪一位來電者

> # May I know who is on the line?
> 請問你的大名？

實用會話

A Hello, can I talk to Mrs. Jones?
哈囉，我要找瓊斯女士說話。

B Yes, madam, may I know who is on the line?
好的，女士，請問你的大名？

A This is Kate White.
我是凱特‧懷特。

B Wait a moment, please.
請稍候！

（轉接中）

B It's for you, Mrs. Jones. It's Ms. White.
瓊斯先生，找你的。是懷特小姐。

C Thanks. Just put her through.
謝謝！把她轉接過來。

相關用語

▶ Who is this, please?
請問你是哪一位？

【Unit 03】口語化詢問來電者身份

> # Who is this?
>
> 你是哪位？

實用會話

A
Hello, may I speak to Tina?
哈囉，我能和蒂娜說話嗎？

B
May I ask who is calling?
請問你是哪位？

A
Paul Jones.
我是保羅‧瓊斯。

B
Hi, Paul! It's me.
嗨，保羅！是我啊！

A
Who is this?
你是哪位？

B
This is Mary, Tina's roommate. Don't you remember me? I met you at the party last week.
我是瑪莉，蒂娜的室友。你不記得我了嗎？上星期的派對上我見過你。

關鍵單字

▶ roommate　住在同室的人、室友、同居者
▶ last　上一次、前一次、最新的

【 Unit 04 】猜測來電者的身份

Is this David?

是大衛嗎？

實用會話

A
Hello?
喂？

B
Hi, may I speak to Mr. Smith?
嗨，我能和史密斯先生說話嗎？

A
Sorry, but he went out for lunch. Is this David?
抱歉，他出去吃午餐了！你是大衛嗎？

B
Yes, this is David Jones.
是的，我是大衛‧瓊斯。

A
Hi, David, this is Tina. Do you remember me?
嗨，大衛，我是蒂娜。你還記得我嗎？

B
Tina? Tina Green? Good to hear your voice. How are you doing?
蒂娜？蒂娜‧葛林？真高興聽見你的聲音。你好嗎？

A
Great. How about you?
還不錯！你好嗎？

【Unit 05】沒認出來電者的聲音

> # I didn't recognize your voice.
> 我沒認出你的聲音。

實用會話

A Hello, is Carol there?
哈囉，請問卡洛在嗎？

B Speaking.
我就是。

A Hi, Carol, I'm sorry to call you so late.
嗨，卡洛，對不起這麼晚打電話給你！

B Who is this?
你是哪位？

A This is Doug.
我是道格。

B Hi, Doug. Sorry, I didn't recognize your voice.
嗨，道格，對不起，我沒認出你的聲音。

關鍵單字

► late (時間)晚地

► recognize 認出、看出、意識到

► voice 聲音、噪音、說話聲

【 Unit 06 】直接認出來電者的身份

David?

（你是）大衛嗎？

實用會話

A
Hello?
喂？

B
Hi, may I speak to Mr. Smith?
嗨，我能和史密斯先生説話嗎？

A
David? This is Tina. John's sister.
（你是）大衛嗎？我是蒂娜，約翰的姊妹。

B
Tina? Hi, I haven't heard from you for a long time. How are you?
蒂娜？嗨，好久沒有你的消息了！你好嗎？

A
Great. Thanks. I heard about you and Kate. I'm really sorry about that.
不錯！謝謝關心！我聽説你和凱特的事了！我感到很遺憾！

B
Don't worry about me. I'll be fine.
不用擔心我！沒事的！

Chapter 4

請來電者稍候

【Unit 01】口語化請來電者稍候

> # Hold on.
> 等一下。

實用會話

A
Four Seasons Motel. Good morning.
四季汽車旅館。早安。

B
May I speak to Mr. Jones?
我能和瓊斯先生說話嗎？

A
Hold on.
等一下。

B
Sure.
好的。

（稍後）

A
I'm sorry, but he's busy with another line.
很抱歉，他正在忙線中。

B
That's all right. I'll try to call him later.
沒關係。我晚一點再打電話給他。

相關用語

▶Hold on a second.

稍等一下。

▶Hold on, please.

請等一下。

【Unit 02】正式地請來電者稍候

Just a minute, please.
請稍候。

實用會話

A Hello, is Carrie there, please?
哈囉，凱莉在嗎？

B Just a minute, please.
請稍候。

A Thank you.
謝謝你。

（稍後）

B I'm afraid she's not here.
她恐怕不在這裡。

A Could you give her a message, please?
你能幫我留話給她嗎？

B Yes, of course.
當然可以。

相關用語

▶Wait a moment, please.
請稍候！

▶Hold on for a while please.
請稍候！

▶Please wait a moment.
請稍候！

▶Hold on, please.
請稍候。

【Unit 03】詢問來電者是否願意稍候

Would you please wait a moment?
能請你稍候嗎？

實用會話

A China Airlines. What can I help you with?
中國航空。我能你效勞嗎？

B I want to talk to Mr. Johnson.
我想和強森先生說話。

A May I ask who is calling?
我能請教你的名字嗎？

B This is Peter, one of his friends, calling from New York.
我是彼得，他的朋友，從紐約打電話來的。

A Would you please wait a moment?
能請你稍候嗎？

B No problem.
沒問題。

相關用語

▶Hold on a second, please.

請稍候！

▶Hang on just a second.

等一下不要掛斷喔！

關鍵單字

▶no problem　沒問題(此為答應的意思)

【Unit 04】請來電者不要掛斷，等候聽電話

Can you hold?

你可以稍候嗎？

實用會話

A Johnson Company. May I help you?
強生公司，可以為你服務嗎？

B Is Mr. Sandler in the office?
山得拉先生在辦公室嗎？

A Let me see if he is in.
我看看他在不在。

B Thank you.
謝謝你。

（稍後）

A Mr. Sandler is on another line. Can you hold?
山得拉先生正忙線中，你可以稍候嗎？

B That's OK. I'll try again later.
沒關係。我晚一點再打來。

相關用語

▶Could I put you on hold for a second?

能否請你稍待片刻？

關鍵單字

▶hold　停留、保留（此為不要掛電話）

【Unit 05】請對方稍候，自己馬上回來

If you'll wait for just a moment, I'll be right with you.

可以請你等一下嗎？我馬上回來。

實用會話

A　Hi, this is David. I'd like to make a reservation.
嗨，我是大衛。我要預約。

B　All right. May I have your name, please?
好的！請問你的大名？

A　Sure. My name is...
可以的。我的名字是…

B　Sorry, sir. If you'll wait for just a moment, I'll be right with you.
先生，抱歉，可以請你等一下嗎？我馬上回來。

A　No problem. I'll wait.
沒問題！我可以等。

Chapter 5

代接電話

【Unit 01】不確定受話方是否在

Let me see if she is in.

讓我確認她在不在。

實用會話

A｜Could I speak to Miss Mary Garcia?
　　我能和瑪莉‧賈西亞小姐説話嗎？

B｜Let me see if she is in.
　　我看看她在不在。

（稍後）

B｜I'm sorry. She's out to lunch.
　　很抱歉，她出去用午餐了。

A｜Oh, that's not good.
　　喔，那真糟糕！

B｜Would you like to leave a message?
　　你要留言嗎？

A｜No, I'll try to call her later.
　　不用，我會試著晚一點再打電話給她。

B｜OK. She'll be back after 2 o'clock.
　　好的。她兩點鐘以後才會回來。

相關用語

▶I'm not sure if she is in.

我不確定她在不在。（適用於受話方為女性）

關鍵單字

▶ out to lunch　外出用餐

▶ after　之後、在~之後

【Unit 02】代為確認受話方是否在辦公室內

I'll find out if he's in the office.

我看看他是不是在辦公室裡。

實用會話

A
Is Brian in the office now?
布萊恩現在在辦公室嗎？

B
Hold on, please. I'll find out if he's in the office.
請稍等，我看看他是不是在辦公室裡。

A
Thank you.
謝謝你。

（稍後）

B
He's in the office now. I'll put you through to him immediately.
他現在正在辦公室。我立刻幫你轉給他。

A
Thank you.
謝謝！

關鍵單字

▶ office　辦公室、工作場所

▶ find out　查出、尋找、確認

▶ immediately　立即地、馬上地、即刻地

109

【Unit 03】是否要找特定受話方

> # Who in particular would you like to talk to?
>
> 你要找特定的人接電話嗎?

實用會話

A
May I speak to Harvey?
我能和哈維說話嗎?

B
I'm sorry, but he's off today.
很抱歉,他今天休假。

A
Oh, no.
喔!糟糕。

B
Who in particular would you like to talk to?
你要找特定的人接電話嗎?

A
I'd like to talk to Dan.
我要和丹說話。

B
Wait a minute, please. I'll put your call through.
請稍候。我替你轉電話。

關鍵單字

▶ off　不工作的、休息的、(時間)空閒的
▶ particular　特殊的、特別的、特定的、特指的

【Unit 04】詢問要找哪一位受話方

> # Which one do you want to talk to?
> 你要找的是哪一位？

實用會話

A May I speak to David?
我能和大衛說話嗎？

B Which one do you want to talk to?
你要找的是哪一位大衛？

A Pardon?
你說什麼？

B There are two Davids here.
這裡有兩個大衛。

A Oh. I see. I'd like to talk to David Smith.
喔，我瞭解。我要和大衛‧史密斯說話。

B Hold on, please.
請稍候。

相關用語

▶ We have 3 Davids in the house.
我們這裡有三個叫大衛的。

關鍵單字

▶ which 哪一個
▶ pardon 請再說一遍

【Unit 05】代為確認受話方是否願意接電話

I'll see if he's ready to talk to you.
我看看他是不是準備好要和你講(電)話。

實用會話

A Hello, Mr. Brown, is Kevin at home?
哈囉，布朗太太，凱文在家嗎？

B I'll see if he's ready to talk to you.
我看看是不是準備好要和你講(電)話。

A Thank you, Mr. Brown.
謝謝你，布朗太太。

（稍後）

B I'm sorry, Miranda, but he's still upset now.
很抱歉，米蘭達，他現在心情還是很糟。

A But I really have to apologize to...
但是我真的必須道歉…

B You'd better not call him anymore.
你最好不要再打電話給他。

關鍵單字

▶ at home　在家
▶ apologize　道歉

【Unit 06】代為確認受話方是否有空接電話

> ### Let me see if he is available.
> 我看看他現在有沒有空。

實用會話

A　Can I speak to Dr. Howard, please?
　　我能和華德教授說話嗎？

B　Wait a moment, please. Let me see if he is available.
　　請稍候。我看看他現在有沒有空。

A　Sure.
　　好的。

（稍後）

B　He's busy with another line.
　　他現在正在忙線中。

A　That's OK. I'll call back later.
　　沒關係。我晚一點再打來。

B　I'm afraid he won't be free until 3 o'clock.
　　他恐怕三點鐘前都不會有空。

關鍵單字

▶ available (對於接見人、接受工作)有暇的、有空的
▶ another　又一、再一
▶ free　自由的、自主的、不受約束的
▶ until　直到~時(時間的延續)、在~之前、直到~(才)

Chapter 6

轉接電話

【Unit 01】請求轉接電話給受話方

Could you put me through to David, please?

請幫我轉接電話給大衛。

實用會話

A This is Mr. White's office. May I help you?
這是懷特先生的辦公室。可以為你服務嗎？

B Could you put me through to David, please?
請幫我轉接電話給大衛。

A May I know who is speaking?
請問你的大名？

B This is John Jones.
我是約翰‧瓊斯。

A OK, Mr. Jones, I'll put you through to him.
好的，瓊斯先生，我來幫你轉接電話給他。

B Thanks a lot.
多謝啦！

相關用語

▶ Could you transfer me to his line?
可以請你幫我轉接電話給他嗎？

▶ Please connect me to the manager's office.
請幫我轉接到經理的辦公室。

【 Unit 02 】轉接來電者的電話

I'll put you through to her.
我來幫你轉接電話給她。

實用會話

A May I speak with Kate, please?
我能和凱特説話嗎？

B May I know who is speaking?
請問你的大名？

A This is John calling from Taipei.
我是從台北打電話來的約翰。

B OK. Hang on just a second. I'll put you through to her.
好的！請稍等。我來幫你轉接電話給她。

相關用語

▶I'll put you through to her right away.

我馬上幫你轉接電話給她。

▶I'll connect you.

我幫你轉接！

▶I'll put you through.

我幫你轉接！

▶OK. I'll transfer your call now. Hold on.

好的，我現在幫你轉接電話！不要掛斷！

【Unit 03】告知來電者會請受話方來接電話

I'll get her.
我去叫她。

實用會話

A
May I speak to Alice, please?
我能和愛莉絲說話嗎？

B
Hold on, please. I'll get her.
請稍等，我去叫她。

（轉接中）

C
Hello?
喂？

A
Hi, Alice. This is Mark.
嗨，愛莉絲，我是馬克。

C
Hi, Mark, what's up?
嗨，馬克，有什麼事？

相關用語

▶I'll get him.

我去叫他（來聽電話）。（適用受話方為男性）

▶I'll connect you to him.

我幫你轉接電話給他！（適用受話方為男性）

▶I'll go and get Alice for you.

我幫你去叫愛莉絲來接電話！

▶I'll put Alice on.

我去叫愛莉絲來接電話！

【 Unit 04 】轉告受話方有來電待接

> ### I've put him on hold.
> 我已經請他稍候。

實用會話

A
Stanley, there's an Anthony on the phone who wants to talk to you.
史丹立，有一個安東尼在線上，他想和你說話。

B
I'm busy at the moment. Can you ask him to hold?
我現在正在忙。你能請他稍候嗎？

A
Want me to tell him anything first? I've put him on hold.
需要我先告訴他什麼事嗎？我已經請他稍候。

B
Tell him I'll talk with him in a few seconds.
告訴他我會馬上和他說話。

A
Sure. He's on line 2.
好的！他在二線。

B
Thanks, Cathy.
謝謝你，凱西。

相關用語

▶There's a call for you on line one.

一線有你的電話！

▶You have a call on line two.

二線有你的電話！

【Unit 05】告知受話方特定來電者的電話待接

It's your husband on the line.
你的先生在線上（待接）。

實用會話

A Hi, Judy, may I speak to Kate?
嗨，茱蒂，我要找凱特說話。

B Hold on a second. Mr. Smith.
請稍等，史密斯先生！

（轉接中）

B Mrs. Smith, it's your husband on the line.
史密斯太太，你的先生在線上（待接）。

C OK. Put him through.
好的，幫他轉接過來

B Yes, Mrs. Smith.
好的，史密斯太太！

相關用語

▶ Your husband is calling for you.
你的先生打電話找你！

▶ You have a call from Mrs. Miller of Empire marketing Company.
帝國行銷公司的米勒女士打電話給你。

▶ There's a call for you from Mrs. Miller of Empire marketing Company.
帝國行銷公司的米勒女士打電話給你。

【Unit 06】告知受話方有緊急電話待接

He says it's urgent.

他説是急事。

實用會話

A	Excuse me, Mr. Gates, Dr. Ross is on line 3. 抱歉，蓋茲先生，羅斯博士在三線。
B	I asked you to hold all calls for me, didn't I? 我告訴過你幫我留話，不是嗎？
A	But he wants to speak with you. He says it's urgent. 但是他想要和你説話，他説是急事。
B	Get him to call me back tomorrow. 叫他明天再打電話給我。

(稍後A與C對話)

A	I'm sorry, Dr. Ross, Mr. Gates doesn't want to answer the calls during meeting. 很抱歉，羅斯博士，蓋茲先生不想在開會時接電話。
B	I see. When should I call back then? 我了解。那我應該什麼時候打電話過來？

【Unit 07】感謝來電者久候

> # Thank you for waiting.
> 謝謝你等這麼久。

實用會話

A
Hello?
喂?

B
What keeps you so long?
怎麼這麼久才來接電話?

A
Thank you for waiting. I was just in the bathroom.
謝謝你等這麼久。我剛剛在洗手間裡。

B
OK. What?
好吧!什麼?

A
What what?
什麼東西「什麼」?

B
You didn't say anything? It's strange. I heard some unusual noise.
你沒說話嗎?真奇怪,我聽到一些不尋常的聲音。

關鍵單字

▶ keep 繼續、防止、不讓~接近

▶ strange 怪異、奇怪、不尋常

▶ unusual 異常的、不尋常的、奇異的

▶ noise 喧嘩聲、嘈雜聲、吵鬧、騷動

【Unit 08】向來電者致歉久候

> # Sorry to have kept you waiting.
> 抱歉讓你久等了。

實用會話

A Mom? I'm back.
媽？我回來了。

B Are you still busy?
你還在忙？

A No, I'm not. Sorry to have kept you waiting.
我沒有。抱歉讓你久等了。

B That's OK. Did you call your father yesterday?
沒有關係。你昨天有打電話給你爸嗎？

A No, I didn't. What happened to him?
我沒有。他怎麼了？

B He wants to visit you next week.
他想要下個星期去拜訪你。

關鍵單字

▶ yesterday 昨天
▶ happen 使(某事)發生、引發(某事)
▶ visit 訪問、拜訪
▶ week 一整個星期

Chapter 7

受話方
暫時不會回來

【Unit 01】受話方在上班中

He's at work.

他去上班了！

實用會話

A
Hello?
喂？

B
Hello, is John there?
哈囉，約翰在嗎？

A
No, he is not here right now. He's at work.
不在，他現在不在這裡。他去上班了！

B
I see. Is David there?
我瞭解！大衛在嗎？

A
Yes, he is. Hang on a second.
是的，他在。等一下。

B
Thanks.
謝謝！

相關用語

►Oh, he is not in. May I take a message?
喔，他不在！我可以留話嗎？

【Unit 02】受話方暫時不在

> ### He's not in yet.
> 他現在還不在。

實用會話

A May I speak to Dr. Lee, please?
我能和李醫生說話嗎？

B I'm sorry. He's not in yet. Would you care to leave a message?
好抱歉，他還沒有進來。你要留言嗎？

A No. Thanks. Do you have any idea where he is right now?
不用，謝謝。你知道他現在人在哪裡嗎？

B He's probably on his way home.
他可能在回家的路上。

A On his way home? I'll call him at home.
回家的路上？我打電話到他家給他。

B Do you have his home number?
你有他家裡的電話嗎？

A Yes, I do.
有的，我有（他的電話）！

相關用語

►He's not here.
他不在。

►He's out now.
他現在出去了！

關鍵單字

▶ on one's way home　在(某人)回家的路上
▶ home number　家裡的電話

【Unit 03】受話方可以接電話的時間

> # He won't be free until ten thirty.
> 他要到十點卅分之後才會有空。

實用會話

A
GQ Magazine. May I help you?
GQ雜誌。可以為你服務嗎？

B
May I speak to the chief editor?
我能和主編說話嗎？

A
Sorry, sir, he won't be free until ten thirty.
先生，很抱歉，他要到十點卅分之後才會有空。

B
Would you ask him to call Mark at 86473663?
你能請他打電話到86473663給馬克嗎？

A
I'd be glad to.
我很樂意。

B
Thank you so much.
非常謝謝你。

關鍵單字

▶ chief editor　主編

▶ glad　高興、雀躍、樂意

【 Unit 04 】詢問受話方回來的時間

When will he be back?

他什麼時候會回來？

實用會話

A
Is John around?
約翰在嗎？

B
I'm sorry, but he's not in the office because he flew to France.
好抱歉，他現在不在辦公室，因為他去法國了。

A
When will he be back?
他什麼時候會回來？

B
Let me check his calendar. Hmm...he'll be back next week.
我查一查他的行事曆，嗯…他下星期才會回來。

A
Well, I guess I'll have to wait until he returns. I'll call again next week.
這個嘛，我猜我應該要等到他回來。我下星期再打電話。

B
Or would you care to leave him a message?
或是你要留言給他？

A
Could you ask him to send me the new products list?
能請你要求他將新的商品清單寄給我嗎？

關鍵單字

▶ check　確認、檢查、求證

【Unit 05】告知來電者受話方回來的時間

He should be back in half an hour.

他應該半個鐘頭後才會回來。

實用會話

A　Hello, may I speak to John Smith?
　　喂，我能和約翰·史密斯説話嗎？

B　I'm sorry. He's out to dinner. Would you like to leave a message?
　　很抱歉。他出去吃晚餐了。你要留言嗎？

A　He's out to dinner? What time do you expect him back?
　　他出去吃晚餐了？你預期他什麼時候會回來？

B　He should be back in half an hour.
　　他應該半個鐘頭後才會回來。

A　I'll try again later. Thank you.
　　我晚一點再試。謝謝你。

B　You are welcome.
　　不客氣。

關鍵單字

▶ expect　預期、期待

▶ in　在～期間、在一段時間之中、在一段時間之後

【Unit 06】受話方正在忙線中

She's busy with another line.
她正在另一條線上講電話。

實用會話

A
May I talk to Jenny Willard, please?
我能和珍妮・葳沃德說話嗎？

B
I'm sorry, but she's busy with another line.
很抱歉，她正在另一條線上講電話。

A
Oh, it's not good.
喔！真糟糕。

B
May I tell her who is calling?
需要我告訴她是誰來電嗎？

A
I am Chuck. Tell her to call me back as soon as possible.
我是查克，告訴她盡快回我電話。

B
May I have your last name, please?
請問你的姓氏是什麼？

A
Gray, Chuck Gray.
葛瑞，查克・葛瑞。

相關用語

▶She's on another line right now.
她現在在另一線忙線中。

▶I'm sorry, but her line is busy now.
抱歉，她現在正在忙線中。

▶I'm sorry but she's not available this time.

抱歉，她現在沒有空。

關鍵單字

▶ as soon as possible 盡快、一旦~就~

▶ last name 姓氏

【Unit 07】告知來電者受話方還在忙線中

She's still on the phone.
她還在講電話。

實用會話

A　Hi, Ms. Max, this is David again. Is Monica there?
嗨，麥斯小姐，我是大衛，我又打電話來了。莫妮卡在嗎？

B　Wait a moment, please.
請等一下。

（稍後）

B　She's still on the phone.
她還在講電話。

A　Hmm...would you tell her to answer my call first? This is urgent.
嗯，可以請你轉告她先接我的電話嗎？這是急事。

B　Sure. I'll ask her. Hold on.
好的，我問她，等一下。

A　Thank you so much.
非常感謝你。

【Unit 08】電話佔線中的時間

> ### The line has been busy for an hour.
> 電話已經佔線一個小時了。

實用會話

A	Is Maria off the line? 瑪麗亞講完電話了嗎？
B	I don't think so. She's still talking to her boyfriend. 我不這麼認為。她還在和她男朋友講電話。
A	The line has been busy for an hour. 電話已經佔線一個小時了。
B	Would you like to leave her a message? 你要留言給她嗎？
A	Sure. Tell her to give David a call as soon as possible. 好！告訴她盡快回大衛電話。
B	I will. 我會的。

關鍵單字

► off the line　離開電話、講完電話
► for an hour　持續一個小時的時間

【Unit 09】詢問如何聯絡受話方

Do you know where I can reach him?

你知道我在哪裡可以聯絡上他嗎？

實用會話

A
Can I speak to Mr. Smith?
我能和史密斯先生說話嗎？

B
I'm afraid he won't be back before four o'clock.
他恐怕在四點鐘之前不會回來。

A
Do you know where I can reach him? It's really urgent.
你知道我在哪裡可以聯絡上他嗎？這件事很緊急。

B
Maybe you can call him at home.
也許你可以打電話到家裡給他。

A
Could you give me the number?
你能給我電話嗎？

B
It's 86473663.
是 86473663。

相關用語

▶Is there any other way I can reach him?
有沒有其他辦法可以聯絡到他？

關鍵單字

▶reach 聯絡

Chapter 8

稍後會再來電

【Unit 01】本人現在無法講電話

I can't talk to you now.
我現在不能講（電話）。

實用會話

A	Would you hold on, please? The baby is crying now.
	你能等一下嗎？小嬰兒正在哭。
B	OK.
	好！
	（稍後）
A	I can't talk to you now.
	我現在不能講電話了。
B	What happened? How is the baby?
	發生什麼事？小嬰兒怎麼了？
A	I don't know. She keeps crying. I'll have to call you back.
	我不知道。她一直不停地哭。我等一下再撥電話給你。
B	Got it. Talk to you later.
	知道了，待會兒再聊。

關鍵單字

▶ baby　嬰兒、寶貝

▶ crying　哭泣

▶ got it　知道、了解、知曉

【Unit 02】詢問可以再來電的時間

When should I call back?
我什麼時候再打來好呢？

實用會話

A Can I talk to Ms. Karras?
我能和凱瑞斯女士說話嗎？

B I'm sorry, but Ms. Karras is in a meeting right now.
很抱歉，凱瑞斯女士正在開會。

A OK. When should I call back?
好吧。那我什麼時候再打來好呢？

B I think the meeting should be over by two o'clock.
我認為會議會在兩點鐘前結束。

A Would you tell her Jack returned her call? And I'll call her later.
請你告訴她傑克回過電話好嗎？我等一下會再打給她。

B Sure. I'll give her this message.
好的，我會告訴她留言。

關鍵單字

► over 結束了、完了、過去了
► by 到~之前、不遲於(時間、期限)
► return 回覆、回答

【Unit 03】稍後會再來電

I'll just call back later.
我稍後會再打電話來。

實用會話

A Hello, this is Mr. Garcia's office.
哈囉,賈西亞先生辦公室。

B Hello, may I speak to Mr. Garcia, please?
哈囉,我能和賈西亞先生說話嗎?

A I'll put you through to Mr. Garcia. Hold on, please.
我幫你轉接給賈西亞先生,請稍候。

(稍後)

A He's not in his office right now. Is this Mr. White? Would you care to leave a message?
他現在不在辦公室。你是懷特先生嗎?你要不要留言?

B No, thank you. I'll just call back later.
不用,謝謝你,我稍後會再打電話來。

A OK. He'll be back by three o'clock.
好的。他三點鐘會回來。

B I see. Thank you.
我了解了,謝謝你。

【 Unit 04 】會嘗試再打電話來

> ### I'll try again later.
> 我待會再試(著撥電話)。

實用會話

A May I help you?
可以為你服務嗎？

B Yes, I want to talk to Mr. Brown. This is Jack White.
是的，我要和布朗先生說話。我是傑克‧懷特。

A Hold on, please. I'll put you through.
請稍等。我幫你轉接。

B Thank you.
謝謝你。

（稍後）

A I'm sorry, Mr. White, Mr. Brown is on another line.
很抱歉，懷特先生，布朗先生正在另一線電話中。

B I'll try again later.
我待會再試(著撥電話)。

相關用語

▶I'll call back later.

我晚一點再打來。

【Unit 05】過幾分鐘會再打來

Let me get back to you in a few minutes.

我幾分鐘後回你電話。

實用會話

A
Pamela, can you come to a meeting on Friday?
潘蜜拉，你星期五能參加會議嗎？

B
I'm not sure. Let me check my schedule. When are you having it?
我不確定，讓我查查我的行程。會議在幾點鐘？

A
We're planning on having it around noon.
我們計劃在中午舉行會議。

B
Let me get back to you in a few minutes.
我幾分鐘後回你電話。

A
Sure. If I'm not in, could you leave a message on my answering machine?
好啊！如果我不在，你能留言在我的答錄機嗎？

B
Sure thing.
沒問題。

關鍵單字

► schedule 進度表、時間表
► planing on 打算、指望
► answering machine 電話答錄機
► sure thing 毫無疑問的事情

【Unit 06】過一個小時之後再來電

Could you call her back in an hour?

你可以一個小時之後再打電話給她嗎？

實用會話

A Hello?
哈囉？

B Hello, Mrs. Jones. This is David.
哈囉，瓊斯太太。我是大衛。

A Hi, David. How are you?
嗨，大衛。你好嗎？

B I'm fine, thanks. Is Betty there?
我很好，謝謝關心。貝蒂在嗎？

A She's eating dinner right now. Could you call her back in an hour?
她現在在吃晚餐。你可以一個小時之後再打電話給她嗎？

B Sure, Mrs. Jones.
好的，瓊斯太太。

【Unit 07】過幾分鐘後再來電

You can try again in a few minutes.
你可以過幾分鐘再打來看看。

實用會話

A May I speak to Vicky?
我能和維琪說話嗎？

B She was here a moment ago.
她剛剛還在這裡。

A When do you expect her back?
你知道她什麼時候會回來嗎？

B I'm not sure, but you can try again in a few minutes.
不清楚，不過你可以過幾分鐘再打來看看。

A But I'm out of office later...
但是我等一下會離開辦公室…

B Oh wait, she just came in.
喔，等一下，她剛進來。

相關用語

▶ You can call back in 10 minutes.
你可以十分鐘後再打來。

關鍵單字

▶ a moment ago　剛剛、前不久
▶ a few　幾個~、一些~
▶ just　剛好、此刻

【Unit 08】詢問來電者是否願意再來電

Would you mind calling back later?

你介不介意待會再打電話來？

實用會話

A
Is Austin in his office? This is Collins Smith calling from Taipei.

奧斯丁在他的辦公室嗎？我是從台北打電話來的柯林斯·史密斯。

B
I'm sorry, but he won't be back until four thirty.

很抱歉，他四點卅分才會回來。

A
Where is he now?

他現在人在哪裡？

B
He went to see a doctor. Would you mind calling back later, Mr. Smith?

他去看醫生了。史密斯先生，你介不介意待會再打電話來？

A
OK. I'll call him by five.

好的，我五點鐘再打電話給他。

B
I'll tell him you called.

我會告訴他你有打電話來。

關鍵單字

▶ see a doctor 看醫生

▶ mind 介意、在意

【Unit 09】指定打電話的時間

Call me at 86473663 after ten.

十點鐘以後打電話到 86473663 給我。

實用會話

A Then I'll call John tomorrow to make sure.
那麼我明天會打電話給約翰做確定。

B OK. Call me as soon as you figure it out.
好。等你知道後要馬上打電話給我。

A I will.
我會的。

B And I won't be in tomorrow.
還有，我明天不在。

A Where are you going?
你要去哪裡？

B Visiting one of my friends. You can call me at 86473663 after ten.
拜訪一個朋友。你可以十點鐘以後打電話到 86473663 給我。

相關用語

▶ Try to give me a call at nine o'clock.
試著在九點鐘打電話給我。

關鍵單字

▶ make sure 確定、確認
▶ visiting 拜訪
▶ one of~ 其中一個~

Chapter 9

詢問來電者是否需要留言

【 Unit 01 】詢問來電者是否要留言

> ### Would you care to leave a message?
>
> 你要留言嗎？

實用會話

A When do you expect him back?
你預期他什麼時候會回來？

B I'm sorry I don't know. Would you care to leave a message?
很抱歉我不知道。你要留言嗎？

A Could you tell him that John Smith called and have him call me back tomorrow?
能請你告訴他約翰・史密斯有來電，也請他明天打電話給我嗎？

B Sure. May I have your phone number?
好的。請給你的電話。

A I think he has my number.
我認為他有我的電話。

B OK. I'll tell him you called.
好的。我會告訴他你有打電話過來。

相關用語

▶ Would you like to leave a message?
你要留言嗎？

▶ Any messages for him?
有沒有要給他的留言？

關鍵單字

▶ phone number 電話號碼

▶ think 認為

【Unit 02】替來電者記下留言

May I take a message?
需要我(替你)留言嗎?

實用會話

A Extension 747.
請接分機747。

B Hold on, please.
請稍候。

(轉接中)

B I'm sorry. She's in a meeting right now. May I take a message?
很抱歉,她現在在開會中。需要我替你留言嗎?

A Sure. Could you please tell her that Maria called? My phone number is 86473663.
好的,能請你告訴她瑪麗亞打電話來嗎?我的電話是 86473663。

B I'll tell her that you called and will have her get back to you as soon as possible.
我會告訴她你打電話給她,也會請她盡快回你電話。

A Thank you so much.
非常謝謝你。

B Sure thing.
應該的。

【Unit 03】準備紙筆寫下留言

Let me get a pencil and paper.
讓我拿一下紙筆。

實用會話

A
May I speak to Rita? This is Tracy.
我能和瑞塔說話嗎？我是崔西。

B
I'm sorry, but she's out to lunch. Would you like to leave a message?
很抱歉，她出去用午餐了。你要留言嗎？

A
OK. Tell her to give me a call. Here is my work number...
好，告訴她回我電話，我的公司電話是…

B
Hold on, let me get a pencil and paper. OK. Go ahead.
等一下，讓我拿一下紙筆。好了，請說。

A
86473663.
86473663．

B
86473663. OK. I'll ask her to call you back.
86473663。好的，我會請她回你電話。

關鍵單字

▶ give someone a call　打電話給某人

▶ go ahead　繼續

【Unit 04】確認來電者的電話

Does she have your number?

她知道你的號碼嗎？

實用會話

A This is John calling from Japan. May I speak to Maria?
我是日本打電話來的約翰，我能和瑪麗亞說話嗎？

B I'm sorry, but she's not at her desk.
很抱歉，她不在她的位子上。

A Can I leave a message? Please ask her to call me back.
我能留言嗎？請她回我電話。

B Does she have your number?
她有你的電話嗎？

A I think so, but just in case, it's 86473663.
我認為她有，不過為了以防萬一，電話是86473663。

B OK, I'll give her the message.
好的，我會把留言給她。

關鍵單字

► in case 以防萬一

► give 給予、託付、委託、移交、交給

【Unit 05】留言在答錄機中

> ### You can leave a message on the answering machine.
>
> 你可以在答錄機裡留言。

實用會話

A
Jeff, are you going home tonight?
傑夫，你今晚要回家嗎？

B
I'm not sure. I might have dinner with my friends. Why?
我不確定，我可能會和我朋友去吃晚餐。怎麼了？

A
I'll call you to talk about your new book.
我會打電話給你討論你新書的事。

B
You can call me at home any time.
任何時候你都可以打電話到我家。

A
What if you are not in?
假如你不在家呢？

B
You can leave a message on the answering machine.
你可以在答錄機留言。

關鍵單字

▶ tonight　今晚
▶ might　也許、可能(表示可能)
▶ any time　任何時候、任何時間
▶ what if　假如～該如何

【 Unit 06 】保證受話方會收到留言

I'll make sure he gets the message.

我會確定他有收到留言。

實用會話

A	May speak to Tom? This is Helen from Seattle. 我能和湯姆說話嗎？我是西雅圖的海倫。
B	I'm sorry, but he's not here. Would you like to leave a message? 很抱歉，他不在這裡，你要留言嗎？
A	Please ask him to give me a call as soon as possible. 請他盡快打電話給我。
B	Does he have your phone number? 他有你的電話號碼嗎？
A	I don't think so. My office number is 86473663. 我覺得他沒有。我辦公室電話號碼是 86473663。
B	OK, I'll make sure he gets the message. 好的，我會確定他會收到留言。

關鍵單字

▶ office number　辦公室電話、公司電話
▶ get　拿到、收到

【 Unit 07 】 保證會轉達留言

I'll give him the message.

我會把留言轉告他！

實用會話

A Good morning, Mr. Baker's office. May I help you?
早安！這是貝克先生的辦公室。可以為你服務嗎？

B Yes. May I speak to Mr. Baker, please?
是的！我可以和貝克先生講電話嗎？

A I'm sorry, but he's not here yet. May I take a message?
抱歉，他還沒進來。需要我記下留言嗎？

B Yes. Could you ask him to call me back?
好的！可以請他回我電話嗎？

A Sure. I'll give him the message.
好的！我會把留言轉告他！

B Thanks.
謝謝！

A You're welcome.
不客氣！

相關用語

►I'll tell him.

我會告訴他！

►I'll tell her.

我會告訴她。

【 Unit 08 】保證請受話方打電話給來電者

I'll have him call you back as soon as possible.

我會請他盡快回你電話。

實用會話

A　May speak to Charlie?
我能和查理說話嗎？

B　I'm sorry, but he's just stepped out.
很抱歉，他剛離開。

A　Well...when do you expect he might come back?
這個嘛…你預期他什麼時候會回來？

B　A couple minutes, maybe.
也許幾分鐘後吧。

A　Could you tell him to give Bell a call when he gets back?
你能告訴他回來時打電話給貝兒嗎？

B　Sure. I'll have him call you back as soon as possible.
當然，我會請他回來時盡快回你電話。

關鍵單字

► a couple　幾個～

► maybe　或許、也許、極有可能

► get back　回到(某處)(此為打電話給對方)

【Unit 09】保證會請受話方回電

I'll have her return your call.
我會請她回你電話。

實用會話

A
Helen? Is Jane around?
海倫嗎？珍在嗎？

B
Hi, Mr. Brown. Mrs. Brown was out to a meeting.
嗨，布朗先生。布朗太太出去開會了。

A
When will she come in?
她什麼時候會回來？

B
Let me check her calendar. It's about 3 o'clock.
我查一下她的日曆。大概三點鐘。

A
Tell her to give me a call when she is in.
她回來時告訴她回我電話。

B
OK. I'll have her return your call.
好的，我會請她回你電話。

關鍵單字

▶ about 大約、大概、接近

【Unit 10】聯絡的方法

How can he get in touch with you?

他要怎麼和你聯絡？

實用會話

A
I want to talk to Dr. Dow.
我要和道爾博士說話。

B
I'm sorry, but he said he's in the middle of something.
很抱歉，他說他現在正在忙。

A
Well, ask him to give me a call when he's available.
好吧！請他有空時打個電話給我。

B
How can he get in touch with you?
他要怎麼和你聯絡？

A
My office number is 86473663.
我的公司電話是 86473663。

B
OK. I'll have him call you back.
好的，我會請他回你電話。

相關用語

▶Does he have your phone number?

他有你的電話嗎？

關鍵單字

▶get in touch　連絡、聯繫(某人)

Chapter 10

和電話留言相關的用語

【Unit 01】預先留言給來電者

> ### If David calls, tell him to be ready at seven.
>
> 如果大衛打電話來，告訴他七點鐘準備好。

實用會話

A I have a lunch meeting with Alex. Please answer the phone for me.
我和艾力克斯有一個午餐約會。請幫我接電話。

B All right, Mr. Litter.
好的，力特先生。

A If David calls, tell him to be ready at seven. I'll pick him up on my way home.
如果大衛打電話來，告訴他七點鐘準備好。我會在回家的路上去接他。

B Sure. I'll tell him to be on time.
好的。我會告訴他要準時。

A And by the way, don't tell anyone my cell phone number.
還有順道一提，不要告訴任何人我的手機號碼。

B Yes sir. And you'd better get going or you will be late.
是的，先生，還有你最好趕快走，否則你會遲到的。

關鍵單字

▶ pick someone up 接某人
▶ on time 準時
▶ by the way 順道一提、順便

【Unit 02】代為打電話

> ### I'll call him for you.
> 我會幫你打電話給他。

實用會話

A
What time is it now?
現在幾點?

B
It's almost three thirty.
快要三點半了。

A
Three thirty? I'd call the dentist. I have an appointment with him at four.
三點半?我最好打電話給牙醫師,我和他四點鐘有約。

B
I'll call him for you.
我會幫你打電話給他。

A
Thank you. Tell him I'm going to be late.
謝謝你。告訴他我會遲到。

B
Come on, you'd better get going now.
快一點,你最好現在趕快走吧!

關鍵單字

► almost   幾乎、快要、接近
► dentist   牙醫師
► come on   快一點、得了吧

【Unit 03】無法回電話

He can't return your call tomorrow.
他明天無法回你電話。

實用會話

A　Any calls for me?
　　有我的電話嗎？

B　Yes, Bill called two hours ago.
　　有的，比爾兩個小時前有打過電話來。

A　What did he say?
　　他有說什麼嗎？

B　He said that he can't return your call to-morrow.
　　他說他明天無法回你電話。

A　Why? What's the matter with him?
　　為什麼？他怎麼了？

B　He said he would be occupied all day.
　　他說他(明天)整天都會很忙。

關鍵單字

▶ hour　一個小時
▶ ago　在~之前、以前
▶ matter　事情、問題、根由、原由
▶ be occupied　被佔、充滿(空間、時間)

【Unit 04】詢問是否有自己的留言

> # Any messages for me?
> 有沒有我的留言？

實用會話

A Any messages for me?
有沒有我的留言？

B You have two messages.
你有兩個留言。

A What are they?
是什麼留言？

B The first is from Mr. Blackstone. He called to reschedule tomorrow's 9:00 meeting for next Tuesday.
第一個是布萊克史東先生，他打電話來重新安排明天九點鐘的會議到下星期二。

A I see. Tell him that's fine by me. What's another one?
我了解，告訴他我沒意見。另一個呢？

B Another message is from Mr. Smith. He asked you to call him back.
另一個留言是史密斯先生，他請你回電話給他。

相關用語

▶ Did I get any phone calls while I was in the meeting?
我開會的時候有沒有找我的電話？

► Any phone calls during the meeting?
會議期間有沒有來電？
► Did I get any phone calls?
有我的電話嗎？
► Did anybody call me?
有人打電話給我嗎？

關鍵單字
► reschedule　重新計畫安排

【Unit 05】詢問某人是否有來電

> ### Did Mr. Smith call me?
> 史密斯先生有打電話給我嗎？

實用會話

A
Good afternoon, Mr. Jones.
午安！瓊斯先生。

B
Good afternoon, Kate. Did Mr. Smith call me?
午安！凱特。史密斯先生有打電話給我嗎？

A
Yes, he called you this morning.
有的。他今天早上有打電話給你。

B
Did he leave a message?
他有留言嗎？

A
No, he said he would call you again.
沒有，他說他會再打電話給你。

B
All right, I'll call him right now.
好吧！我現在打電話給他。

A
Here's the number.
這是他的電話號碼。

相關用語

▶Did Mr. Smith call me this morning?
史密斯先生今天早上有打電話給我嗎？

【Unit 06】來電者等待回電

He's been expecting your call for 3 days.

他已經等你回電了三天了。

實用會話

A Do I have any calls?
有我的電話嗎？

B Yes, Mr. Lee called. Here is his home number.
有的，李先生打過電話。這是他家裡的電話。

A Thanks. I'll return his call tomorrow.
謝謝，我明天會回他電話。

B Mr. Simon, Mr. Lee said it is urgent.
賽門先生，李先生說是重要的事。

A So what? I'm in the middle of something.
那又怎麼樣？我正在忙。

B He's been expecting your call for 3 days.
他已經等你回電了三天了。

相關用語

▶He wants you to call him back.

他要你回他電話。

▶He's expecting your call.

他在等你的電話。

關鍵單字

▶ in the middle of something　正在忙某事

【Unit 07】確認是否收到留言

Did you get the message I left on your answering machine?
你有收到我留在你答錄機裡的留言嗎？

實用會話

A
Good morning, Miss Lee.
早安，李小姐。

B
Good morning, Mr. Eccles.
早安，依克力斯先生。

A
Did I get any calls yesterday?
昨天有我的留言嗎？

B
No. Did you get the message I left on your answering machine?
沒有！你有收到我留在你答錄機裡的留言嗎？

A
Yeah. Thanks so much! You really saved my life!
有啊！真感謝。你救了我呢！

B
No problem.
不客氣。

關鍵單字

▶ yeah　有、是(口語化說法)

▶ save　拯救、解救、救贖

▶ life　生命、性命(此為誇張的用法，表示非常感謝)

165

【Unit 08】確認會回電

> ### I'll give them a call and see what they wanted.
>
> 我會打電話給他們，看看他們有什麼事。

實用會話

A　Did I get any calls?
　　有沒有我的電話？

B　No, but David and John stopped by to see you.
　　沒有，但是大衛和約翰有來找過你。

A　They did? What did they say?
　　他們有來？他們說了什麼？

B　Nothing. They waited a couple of minutes and then left.
　　沒什麼。他們等了幾分鐘，然後就離開了。

A　OK, I'll give them a call and see what they wanted.
　　好的，我會打電話給他們，看看有什麼事。

B　Here is David's new cell phone number.
　　這給你，大衛新的手機號碼。

關鍵單字

▶stopped by　順道訪問、順便(stopped為stop的過去式)

Chapter 11

回電話

【Unit 01】請受話方回電給特定人

Could you please ask her to call Eric?

可以請她打電話給艾瑞克嗎？

實用會話

A
May I speak to David or John, please?
我可以和大衛或是約翰講話嗎？

B
They're not here. Can I give them a message?
他們不在這裡。要留言給他們嗎？

A
No, that's OK. Is Jane there?
沒關係，不用了！珍在嗎？

B
She's at work.
她去上班了。

A
Could you please ask her to call Eric?
可以請她打電話給艾瑞克嗎？

B
OK. I'll tell her.
好的，我會告訴她。

相關用語

▶ Please ask him to give me a call.
請他打電話給我。（適用受話方為男性）

▶ Please ask her to give me a call.
請她打電話給我。（適用受話方為女性）

▶ Just ask David to return my call.
只要請大衛回電給我就好。

【 Unit 02 】打電話給留言者

I'm returning your call.
我現在回你電話。

實用會話

A Hi, Jack, I'm returning your call. What's up?
嗨，傑克，我現在回你電話。什麼事？

B Oh, right! Did you get my message?
喔，對！你有收到我的留言嗎？

A What message? I have no idea about it.
什麼留言？我不知道這件事。

B So you didn't pick up Kathy?
所以你沒有去接凱西？

A Did you leave a message?
你有留言給我嗎？

B Yes. I told your secretary to be sure that you get it.
有，我告訴你的秘書要確定你有收到（留言）。

關鍵單字

► sure　確定無誤的
► returning　回電

【 Unit 03 】詢問對方是否曾經來電

You called me last night, didn't you?
你昨天有打電話給我，不是嗎？

實用會話

A
Stephanie? How is it going?
史蒂芬嗎？你好嗎？

B
Pretty good. How about you?
還不錯。你呢？

A
I'm doing well so far. You called me last night, didn't you?
我目前很好。你昨天有打電話給我，不是嗎？

B
Me? No, I didn't.
我？沒有，我沒有。

A
You didn't? But it sounded like your voice on my answering machine.
你沒有？但是我的答錄機裡(的聲音)聽起來像是你的聲音。

B
I'm so sure that I didn't make that phone call.
我很確定我沒有打那一通電話。

關鍵單字

▶ pretty 　相當的、非常的
▶ so far 　目前為止、迄今為止
▶ sound 　聽起來、令人覺得、似乎

【Unit 04】感謝對方回電

Thank you for returning my call.
謝謝你回我電話。

實用會話

A Mark? This is John.
馬克嗎？我是約翰。

B Thank you for returning my call, John.
謝謝你回我電話，約翰。

A No problem. How do you feel now? I really worry about you.
不客氣！你現在覺得如何？我真的很擔心你。

B I'm fine. I can't believe what Teresa had done to me.
我很好。我不相信泰瑞莎對我所作的事。

A Oh, come on, buddy.
喔！老兄別這樣。

B But I really miss her.
但是我真的很想念她。

相關用語

▶Thank you for calling me back.
謝謝你的回電。

關鍵單字

▶ come on 別這樣、得啦

▶ buddy 好朋友、夥伴、搭檔、老兄

【Unit 05】告知受話方自己有收到留言

I received your message.
我有收到你的留言。

實用會話

A
Hello?
喂？

B
Hi, Kate, it's me Jack.
嗨，凱特，我是傑克。

A
Hi, Jack. When did you come back?
嗨，傑克！你什麼時候回來的？

B
Just now. I received your message. What happened?
剛剛才到。我有收到你的留言。發生什麼事了？

A
You know, it's about David...
你知道的，是有關大衛啦…

相關用語

▶I didn't receive your message.
我沒有收到你的留言。

【Unit 06】告知要回電的留言

> # John suggested giving you a call.
> 約翰建議我打電話給你。

實用會話

A
Could you put me through to Mr. Jones, please?
請幫我轉接(電話)給瓊斯先生。

B
Just a second, please.
請稍候。

(轉接中)

C
Mark here.
我是馬克。

A
This is David. John suggested giving you a call.
我是大衛。約翰建議我打電話給你。

C
Hi, David! John told me about your story last week.
嗨，大衛！約翰上星期告訴我你的事了。

A
I know. He said you are a good friend of his.
我知道。他說你是他的一個好朋友。

關鍵單字

▶ suggested 建議、推薦 (suggest的過去式)

Chapter 12

電話打不通

【Unit 01】電話佔線中

> # I kept getting a busy signal.
> 我一直聽到佔線中的嘟嘟聲。

實用會話

A Why didn't you call me yesterday?
你昨天為什麼不打電話給我？

B I tried to, but I couldn't get through.
我有嘗試(打電話給你)，可是我撥不通。

A What time did you call?
你什麼時候打的電話？

B I tried all morning.
我試了一個早上。

A Then I can't understand why you couldn't get through.
那我就不懂為什麼你會撥不通？

B I kept getting a busy signal.
我一直聽到佔線中的嘟嘟聲。

關鍵單字

▶ get through　撥通電話
▶ understand　理解、瞭解、明白
▶ signal　訊號聲

【Unit 02】電話無法接通

It's so difficult to get through!
電話很難接通。

實用會話

A
Did you call Ben last night?
你昨天晚上有打電話給班嗎？

B
Yes. I tried to call him last night, but it's so difficult to get through.
是的，我有試著打電話給他，但是電話很難接通。

A
That's strange. Maybe he was on the net.
奇怪了，也許他在上網。

B
No wonder the line was busy all the time! He ought to get another line.
難怪老是佔線。他應該再去申請一條線路。

A
Or he should get call-waiting.
或是他應該申請插撥。

B
That's a good idea!
好主意。

關鍵單字

▶ difficult　困難的、不容易的
▶ no wonder　不足為奇、難怪
▶ call-waiting　電話插撥

【Unit 03】說明電話被斷線

> # My telephone was disconnected.
> 我的電話打不通。

實用會話

A What's the matter with your phone, Dale? I tried to call you last night.

戴爾，你的電話怎麼了？我昨天晚上一直試著打電話給你。

B I'm sorry. No one was able to get through yesterday.

對不起，昨天沒有人能撥得通電話。

A What happened?

發生什麼事？

B My telephone was disconnected by the phone company.

我的電話被電話公司斷線。

A Didn't you pay the bill?

你沒付帳單嗎？

B Well...I forgot.

這個嘛…我忘了。

關鍵單字

▶ able~　有能力的、能夠～的
▶ disconnect　使不連接、使分離
▶ pay　還清
▶ bill　帳單、帳款

【Unit 04】話筒沒掛好

Is your phone off the hook?
你的話筒有掛好嗎？

實用會話

A Why didn't you call me yesterday?
你昨天為什麼不打電話給我？

B I tried calling you all night.
我整個晚上都試著打電話給你。

A Really?
真的？

B But I can't get through. Is your phone off the hook?
但是我一直無法撥通。你的話筒有掛好嗎？

A I don't think so.
應該有掛好。

B Why are you so sure?
為什麼你這麼確定？

關鍵單字

▶ off 離開的、脫掉的、不接觸的
▶ hook 話筒上的連接掛勾

【Unit 05】詢問電話是否被停話

Is your phone out of order?
你的電話停話中嗎？

實用會話

A Is your phone out of order?
你的電話停話中嗎？

B What do you mean?
你什麼意思？

A I tried calling you all last night, but I couldn't get through.
我昨天晚上一直試著打電話給你，但是我撥不通。

B Oh, I was on the phone all night. Sorry about that.
喔，我昨天晚上一直在電話中。對不起。

A Well, you might wanna add call-waiting to your phone service if you're always on the phone
是喔！如果你老是在電話中，你應該要申請插撥服務。

B I guess so.
我也是這樣覺得。

關鍵單字

▶ out of order (裝置) 出故障的

▶ wanna "want to" 的意思，英語裡常將其快速念成 "wanna"

Chapter 13

電話中聽不清楚

【Unit 01】電話線路不良

We seem to have a bad connection on this phone.

我們的電話線路似乎不太好。

實用會話

A
I can hardly hear you, Nick!
尼克，我聽不到你的聲音！

B
Oh, we seem to have a bad connection on this phone.
喔！我們的電話線路似乎不太好。

A
Could you speak louder, please?
能請你大聲一點嗎？

B
I'm talking as loud as I can.
我已應盡量大聲了。

A
I'm going to hang up and call again.
我要掛電話再撥一次。

B
All right!
好。

相關用語

▶ I think the connection is bad.

我覺得電話線路不太好。

關鍵單字

▶ hardly　幾乎不、差不多沒有

【Unit 02】聽不清楚對方的話

Pardon?
你説什麼？

實用會話

A
Night Star Hotel. May I help you?
夜星旅館，可以為你服務嗎？

B
Yes, is Mr. White there?
是的，懷特先生在嗎？

A
I'm sorry, but he is...
很抱歉，他…

(有雜訊干擾以致B聽不清楚)

B
Pardon?
你説什麼？

A
Mr. White is out to dinner.
懷特先生出去用晚餐了。

B
I see. Thank you. I'll call him later.
我了解，謝謝你！我會再打電話給他。

相關用語

▶Can you hear me?

你聽得到我説話嗎？

▶Can you hear me now?

你現在聽得到我説話嗎？

▶I can hardly hear you.

我聽不見你説話。

【Unit 03】請對方再說一遍

> # Say again?
>
> 你再說一遍好嗎？

實用會話

A
May I speak to Nancy?
我能和南西說話嗎？

B
I'm afraid she's not here.
她恐怕不在這裡。

A
Can I leave her a message?
我能留言給她嗎？

B
Sure.
好。

A
Would you have her call me back? My number is....
能請她回我電話嗎？我的電話是…

B
Say again?
你再說一遍好嗎？

A
My phone number is 86473663.
我的電話是 86473663。

關鍵單字

► say again　再說一次(因為聽不清楚對方的話，所以請對方重複一次的意思)

【Unit 04】請對方說大聲一點

Could you speak up?

你可以説大聲一點嗎？

實用會話

A What do you think of my plans?
你覺得我的計畫如何？

B David? Hello? I can't hear you.
大衛？喂？我聽不見你！

A Can you hear me now?
你現在聽得到我説話嗎？

B No. Your voice is very faint. Could you speak up?
聽不到。你的聲音好小！你可以説大聲一點嗎？

A Can I call you back in a few minutes?
我等一下再回電給你吧！

B Sure.
好啊！

相關用語

▶I really can't hear a word you're saying.
我真的聽不見你説的話。

▶Please speak a little louder.
請大聲一點。

關鍵單字

▶ faint　虛弱的、微小的

【 Unit 05 】請對方說慢一點

Could you speak more slowly?

你可以說慢一點嗎？

實用會話

A
Hi, may I speak to Mr. Smith?
嗨，我要找史密斯先生。

B
He just stepped out. May I know who is speaking?
他剛剛才離開。請問你的大名？

A
This is John Jones from BBC Corporation. My phone number is 86473663.
我是BBC公司的約翰‧瓊斯。我的電話號碼是 86473663。

B
Sorry, sir, could you speak more slowly?
先生，抱歉，你可以說慢一點嗎？

【 Unit 06 】因為聽不清楚，請對方再來電

Why don't you hang up and call again?

你要不要掛斷重新再打電話？

實用會話

A
Can you hear me now?
你現在聽得到我說話嗎？

B
Your voice is very faint.
你的聲音好小聲。

A
Maybe it's a bad connection.
線路可能不太好！

B
Why don't you hang up and call again?
你要不要掛斷重新再打電話？

A
OK. I'll call back in a few minutes.
好吧！我等一下再打電話過來。

B
OK. I'll be waiting.
好！我等你電話！

Chapter 14

打錯電話

【 Unit 01 】打錯電話

> # I'm afraid you have the wrong number.
>
> 你可能是打錯電話了。

實用會話

A May I speak to Mr. Martin?
我能和馬丁先生說話嗎？

B I'm afraid you have the wrong number.
你可能是打錯電話號碼了。

A Is this Martin residence?
這是馬丁公館嗎？

B No, it's not.
不是。

A Is this 86473663?
是 86473663 嗎？

B Yes, it is, but this is not Martin residence.
是的，但這不是馬丁公館。

相關用語

▶ I'm sorry, but you've got the wrong number.

抱歉，你打錯電話號碼了！

▶ You must have the wrong number.

你一定是打錯電話號碼了。

關鍵單字

▶ wrong　出故障的、有毛病的、不正常的
▶ residence　住宅、邸宅、住處、居所

【Unit 02】質疑對方可能打錯電話

John? No such person here.
（你要找）約翰？這裡沒有這個人！

實用會話

A
Hello?
喂？

B
Hello, is John there?
哈囉，約翰在嗎？

A
John?
（你要找）約翰？

B
John Hudson.
約翰‧哈德森。

A
No such person here.
沒有這個人！

B
Oh...is this 86473663?
喔…這是 86473663 嗎？

A
No, it's not. I think you have the wrong number.
不，不是！我想你打錯電話號碼了。

B
I'm sorry.
抱歉！

【Unit 03】確認自己撥的電話號碼

> ## I'm calling 86473663.
> 我撥的電話是 **86473663**。

實用會話

A
Is Janet around?
珍妮在嗎？

B
What number did you dial?
你撥幾號？

A
I'm calling 86473663.
我撥的電話是 86473663。

B
There is no one here.
這裡沒有這個人。

A
Is this Dow residence?
這是道爾公館嗎？

B
No, it's not. You must have the wrong number.
不是。你一定是打錯電話號碼了。

關鍵單字

▶ dial　撥電話

【Unit 04】確認對方撥的電話號碼

> # What number are you calling?
> 你打幾號？

實用會話

A May I talk to Charlie, please?
我能和查里說話嗎？

B I'm sorry, but there is no one here by that name.
很抱歉，這裡沒有這個人。

A Is this not Star Company?
這不是星光公司？

B What number are you calling?
你打幾號？

A Is this 86473663?
這是 86473663 嗎？

B No, it's not.
不是。

相關用語

▶ What number are you trying to reach?
你打的電話號碼是幾號？

關鍵單字

▶ company 公司、商號

▶ calling 撥打電話

【Unit 05】詢問是否知道分機號碼

Do you know his extension?
你知道他的分機嗎?

實用會話

A Mr. White's office. May I help you?
這是懷特先生的辦公室。可以為你服務嗎?

B Can I talk to David, please? This is his friend John calling.
我能和大衛說話嗎?我是他的朋友約翰。

A David? Do you know his extension?
大衛?你知道他的分機嗎?

B Sorry. I thought this was his direct line.
抱歉!我以為這是他的專線。

A No problem. Let me look up his extension for you.
沒關係!我幫你查一下他的分機號碼。

B Thanks.
謝謝!

A He's at extension 403. I'll connect you.
他的分機是403。我幫你轉接。

關鍵單字

▶ direct line 專線電話
▶ look up 查詢

【Unit 06】確認來電者要找的人是誰

> # Whom are you trying to reach?
> 你要找誰？

實用會話

A
Is Mr. White there?
懷特先生在嗎？

B
I'm sorry, but he's in a meeting now.
很抱歉，他在開會中。

A
This is David of Happy Travel Company. I want to arrange Mr. White's trip.
我是快樂旅行社的大衛。我想要安排懷特先生的旅程。

B
Both of his secretaries, Mary and Kate, are available; whom are you trying to reach?
他的兩個秘書瑪莉和凱莉都有空，你要找誰？

A
I'd like to talk to Kate.
我要和凱莉說話。

B
Wait a moment, please.
請稍等。

相關用語

▶ Who do you want to talk to?
你要找誰講電話？

▶ Who would you like to talk to?
你要找誰講電話？

【Unit 07】沒有來電要找的人

> **There is no one here by that name.**
> 這裡沒有這個人。

實用會話

A	Hello? 喂？
B	Hi. May I speak to Nancy? 嗨！我能和南西說話嗎？
A	Nancy? I'm sorry, but there is no one here by that name. 南西？很抱歉，這裡沒有（南西）這個人。
B	Sorry. I must have the wrong number. 抱歉！我一定是打錯電話號碼了！
A	It's OK. 沒關係！

相關用語

▶There is nobody here by that name.

這裡沒有這個人。

▶There is nobody named David here.

這裡沒有叫大衛的人。

【Unit 08】公司沒有這個人

> ### There is no Jason Brown in the office.
>
> 辦公室裡沒有傑生‧布朗這個人。

實用會話

A May I speak to Jason Brown?
我能和傑生‧布朗說話嗎?

B Jason Brown? There is no Jason Brown in the office.
傑生‧布朗?辦公室裡沒有傑生‧布朗這個人。

A No Jason Brown? But they gave me this number...
沒有傑生‧布朗?但是他們給我這個號碼…

B What number are you calling?
你撥幾號?

A It's 86473663, extension 403.
是 86473663,分機 403 號。

B I'm afraid you dialed the wrong number.
你恐怕撥錯電話了。

A Really?
真的嗎?

B That's all right. I'll put you through to him.
沒關係。我幫你轉接給他。

【Unit 09】轉接到錯的分機

> **They must have put you through to the wrong extension.**
>
> 他們一定把你轉錯分機了。

實用會話

A
Hello, may I speak to Mr. Smith?
喂，我要找史密斯先生。

B
They must have put you through to the wrong extension.
他們一定把你轉錯分機了。

A
Could you put me through to his line?
你可以幫我轉到他的分機嗎？

B
Certainly. I'll put you through right away.
當然可以！我馬上幫你轉。

A
Thank you so much.
非常感謝！

B
You're welcome. Wait a moment, please.
不客氣！請稍等。

Chapter 15

用電話建立
人際關係

【Unit 01】去電時的問候

I'm calling to say hi.
我打電話來說一聲嗨。

實用會話

A
Hello?
喂？

B
Hi, Kate, it's me.
嗨，凱西，是我。

A
Hi, Jason. Are you all right?
嗨，傑生，你還好吧？

B
I'm fine. Hey, I'm just calling to say hi. How have you been?
我很好，我打只是電話來說一聲嗨！你好嗎？

A
I'm fine. How is John? I miss him so much.
我很好！約翰好嗎？我很想念他！

B
Oh, he's fine.
喔，他很好。

相關用語

▶Long time no see! How have you been?
好久不見！你好嗎？

【Unit 02】因為特別事件的關心問候

> ### I heard you had a car accident the other day.
>
> 我聽說你前幾天出車禍了。

實用會話

A　Hello?
　　喂？

B　Hi, Mark?
　　嗨，馬克嗎？

A　Hi, John. What's up?
　　嗨，約翰，什麼事？

B　I heard you had a car accident the other day. Are you OK?
　　我聽說你前幾天出車禍了。你還好吧？

A　My leg was broken.
　　我的腿摔斷了。

B　That's terrible. How do you feel now?
　　真糟糕！你現在覺得如何？

關鍵單字

► car accident　車禍
► leg　腿
► feel　感覺、意識到

【Unit 03】認出來電者後打招呼

Oh, Tracy. Hi, how are you?
喔，崔西！嗨，你好嗎？

實用會話

A
Hello?
喂？

B
Hello, is Ben there?
哈囉，班在嗎？

A
This is Ben.
我就是！

B
Hi, Ben. This is Tracy.
嗨，班。我是崔西。

A
Tracy?
崔西？

B
Tracy Baker.
崔西・貝克。

A
Oh, Tracy. Hi, how are you?
喔，崔西！嗨，你好嗎？

B
Good, thanks.
很好！謝謝！

【Unit 04】在電話中閒聊

I'm not doing anything special.
我沒在做什麼事!

實用會話

A
Hello?
喂?

B
Jimmy? This is Kate. Can I speak to Eric?
吉米嗎?我是凱特。我可以和艾瑞克說話嗎?

A
Sure. Wait a moment.
好的!等一下。

(轉接中)

C
Hi, Kate.
嗨,凱特!

B
Hi, Eric, what are you doing?
嗨,艾瑞克,你在做什麼?

C
Watching T.V. What about you?
在看電視。你呢?

B
I'm not doing anything special. Hey, look, do you have any plans this weekend?
我沒在做什麼事!嘿,聽著,你這個週末有事嗎?

C
No, why?
沒有!有事嗎?

【Unit 05】直接認出受話方的身份

Hi, Sara, Is that you?

嗨，莎拉，是你嗎？

實用會話

A
Hello?
喂？

B
Hi, Sara, Is that you?
嗨，莎拉，是你嗎？

A
Yes. Who is this?
是啊！你是哪位？

B
It's me, John. I want to ask if you have time to go out for a dinner with me.
我是約翰啊！我要問你有沒有空和我出去吃晚餐。

A
That's a great idea. I'd love to.
好主意！我願意啊！

B
I'll pick you up in about 5 minutes.
我五分鐘後去接你。

A
OK. See you later.
好啊！再見！

相關用語

▶Sara? Hi, it's me, John.
莎拉嗎？是我，約翰。

【Unit 06】提出邀請

Would you like to come over for dinner on Sunday evening?

你星期天晚上要不要過來吃晚餐？

實用會話

A Hello?
喂？

B Hello, Kate. This is Eric.
哈囉，凱特！我是艾瑞克。

A Hi, Eric, what's up?
嗨，艾瑞克，有事嗎？

B Would you like to come over for dinner on Sunday evening?
你星期天晚上要不要過來吃晚餐？

A I'd ove to. What time do you want me to come?
好啊！你要我什麼時候到？

B About six o'clock.
大概六點鐘。

A OK. I'll be there on time.
好啊！我會準時到。

【Unit 07】邀請對方出席

Can you come?
你可以過來嗎？

實用會話

A Hello?
喂？

B Hello, Betty. This is John.
哈囉，貝蒂。我是約翰。

A Oh, hi, John.
喔，嗨，約翰！

B Listen, I'm having a party on Saturday night. Can you come?
是這樣的，我要在星期六晚上辦派對。你可以過來嗎？

A This Saturday or next Saturday?
這個星期六還是下個星期六？

B This Saturday.
這個星期六。

A Sure. What time?
好啊！什麼時間？

【Unit 08】希望和對方談一談

> # We gotta talk.
> 我們必須要聊一聊。

實用會話

A Hello, is this Jennifer?
哈囉，是珍妮佛嗎？

B Yes, speaking.
是的，請説！

A Hi, Jennifer, this is David.
嗨，珍妮佛，我是大衛。

B David! How are you? Where have you been?
大衛！你好嗎？你都去哪裡了？

A Listen, we gotta talk.
聽好，我們必須要聊一聊。

B What happened?
怎麼啦？

相關用語

▶I need to talk to you.

我要和你談一談！

▶Got a minute?

你有空嗎？

【Unit 09】聯絡的方式

How do I contact you?

我要怎麼聯絡你？

實用會話

A
Call me, OK?
打電話給我，好嗎？

B
How do I contact you?
我要怎麼聯絡你？

A
During the daytime, you can reach me at my work number.
白天的時候可以打我公司的電話。

B
I see.
我知道！

A
And in the evenings you can reach me at 0912000222.
晚上的時候打到0912000222就可以聯絡到我。

B
No problem. I'll give you a call sometime.
沒問題！我會打電話給你。

Chapter 16

打國際電話

【 Unit 01 】打國際電話

> ### Have you ever placed calls to America?
> 你曾經打電話到美國嗎？

實用會話

A Linda, can I ask you a question?
琳達，我能問你一個問題嗎？

B Sure. What's up?
當然，什麼事？

A Have you ever placed calls to America?
你曾經打電話到美國嗎？

B I place a call to my husband twice a week. Who are you calling to?
我一個星期打兩次電話給我先生。你要打電話給誰？

A My daughter. She is in New York.
我女兒，她在紐約。

B How often do you call her?
你多常打電話給她？

關鍵單字

► question　疑問、問題
► have you ever　你是否曾經～(做過某事)
► place calls　打電話
► husband　先生、丈夫
► twice　兩次、兩回

【Unit 02】對方付費的國際電話

> ### I'd like to make a collect call to Sydney.
>
> 我要打一通對方付費的電話到雪梨。

實用會話

A Operator. May I help you?
這是總機,可以為你服務嗎?

B Yes, I'd like to make a collect call to Sydney.
是的,我要打一通對方付費的電話到雪梨。

A All right. Is it the station-to-station or person-to-person call?
好的。是不指定收話人還是指定收話人?

B It's person-to-person.
指定收話人。

A OK. What is the name of the person you are calling?
好的。對方的名字是什麼?

B It's George Smith.
是喬治·史密斯。

關鍵單字

▶ operator 接線生、總機
▶ a collect call 對方付費電話
▶ station-to-station (長途電話)叫號的(所撥的號碼接通即開始收費)
▶ person-to-person (長途電話)指定受話人的(指定受話人開始通話後計費)

Chapter 17

打電話的時機

【Unit 01】擔心來電是否吵醒對方

I hope I didn't wake you up.
希望我沒有吵醒你。

實用會話

A Hello, Nancy?
喂，南西嗎？

B Doug! How are you?
道格！你好嗎？

A I hope I didn't wake you up.
希望我沒有吵醒你。

B No, you didn't. I was just watching TV.
你沒有，我只是在看電視。

A I see. Would you like to come over for dinner on Sunday evening?
是這樣喔！你星期天晚上要不要過來吃晚餐？

B Yes, I'd love to. What time do you want me to come?
好啊，我很願意去。你要我什麼時候到？

關鍵單字

► wake 使甦醒、使復活

► come over 順便來訪、傳過來

► evening 傍晚、晚(間) (指日落到就寢間)

【Unit 02】擔心來電是否打擾對方

> # I hope I didn't disturb you.
> 我希望我沒有打擾你。

實用會話

A George here.
我是喬治。

B Hi, George. Do you have a minute now?
嗨，喬治。你現在有空嗎？

A Hey, Joe, what's up?
嘿，喬，什麼事？

B I want to talk to you about my job.
我想要和你談一談有關我的工作。

A What's wrong?
怎麼了？

B I hope I didn't disturb you. I just want to quit.
我希望我沒有打擾你，我只是要辭職。

關鍵單字

▶ disturb　妨礙、妨害、侵害
▶ quit　辭職、離職

【Unit 03】抱歉太晚打電話

I'm sorry to call you so late.
我很抱歉這麼晚打電話給你。

實用會話

A Hello?
喂？

B Hello, Mary?
哈囉，瑪莉嗎？

A This is Mary. What time is it now?
我是瑪莉。現在幾點了？

B It's eleven o'clock. I'm sorry to call you so late.
現在十一點鐘了。我很抱歉這麼晚電話給你。

A What's the big deal?
有什麼重要的事嗎？

B Honey, I'm asking you to marry me.
親愛的，我要你嫁給我。

關鍵單字

▶ time　時光、時間、歲月
▶ deal　事、事件、物品
▶ marry　和～結婚、娶、嫁

【Unit 04】吃飯的時間打電話

I'm sorry to call you at dinner time.

很抱歉吃晚餐的時間打電話過來。

實用會話

A | May I speak with Betty, please?
我能和貝蒂説話嗎？

B | May I know who is speaking?
我能知道你的名字嗎？

A | This is Dennis. I'm sorry to call you at dinner time.
我是丹尼斯。很抱歉吃晚餐的時間打電話過來。

B | No problem. We haven't started eating yet. I'll get her.
沒關係。我們還沒開始吃。我去叫她。

A | Thank you.
謝謝你。

（轉接中）

C | Betty here.
我是貝蒂。

A | Hi, Betty. Got a minute now?
嗨，貝蒂，現在有空嗎？

關鍵單字

► at dinner time　在晚餐的時間
► no problem　沒關係、沒問題
► start　開始

【Unit 05】確定來電的時機是否適宜

> # Am I calling at a bad time?
> 我來電的時機對嗎?

實用會話

A
Hello, may I speak to Mr. Brown?
哈囉,我能和布朗先生說話嗎?

B
This is he.
我就是。

A
Hi, Mr. Brown. Am I calling at a bad time?
嗨,布朗先生,我來電的時機對嗎?

B
It's OK. I'm just listening to the radio.
沒關係!我只是在聽廣播。

A
I have an idea about our new plans.
我有一個點子是關於我們的計畫。

B
Really? That's wonderful.
真的?太好了。

關鍵單字

▶ listen to the radio　聽收音機
▶ have an idea　有一個主意
▶ plan　計畫、方案、設計、方法、辦法

【Unit 06】應該早一點打電話

I should have called earlier.
我應該早一點打電話的。

實用會話

A
May I speak to Mr. Frank Smith, please?
我能和法蘭克・史密斯先生説話嗎?

B
I'm sorry. He has been gone all day.
很抱歉,他今天都不在。

A
Oh, I should have called earlier.
我應該早一點打電話的

B
Would you like to leave a message?
你要留言嗎?

A
Yes. Could you tell him that John called?
是的,你告訴他約翰打過電話來嗎?

B
Certainly.
當然好。

關鍵單字

▶ all the day 終日、一天到晚
▶ earlier 早一點地、提早地

【 Unit 07 】接電話者還沒睡

> ### I'm still up.
> 我還沒睡。

實用會話

A
Hello? Mr. White?
喂？懷特先生嗎？

B
Hi, Tracy! How are you?
嗨，崔西！你好嗎？

A
I'm fine. I'm sorry to call you so late.
我很好。我很抱歉這麼晚打電話給你。

B
That's OK. I'm still up.
沒關係，我還沒睡。

A
I just want to talk about my studying plans.
我只是要討論一下我的讀書計畫。

B
Go ahead.
說吧！

關鍵單字

▶ up 起床的、站著的

【Unit 08】接電話者已經起床

> # I have been up for hours.
> 我已經起床好幾個鐘頭了。

實用會話

A Hello?
喂？

B Linda?
琳達嗎？

A Who is this?
你是哪位？

B This is Bob. I'm sorry to call you so early.
我是鮑伯。我很抱歉這麼早打電話給你。

A That's OK. I have been up for hours. What's up?
沒關係。我已經起床好個鐘頭了。什麼事？

B It's about John. Do you know he is crazy about you?
是關於約翰，你知道他喜歡妳嗎？

關鍵單字

► early 早、先前、最初、早期
► for hours 持續幾個小時
► crazy 狂熱的、熱衷的

【Unit 09】接電話者正要開始工作

> # I'm just ready for work.
> 我準備要工作了。

實用會話

A May I speak to David?
我能和大衛說話嗎？

B Wait a moment, please.
請稍等。

A Sure.
當然。

(轉接中)

C David here.
我是大衛。

A Hi, David, I hope I didn't interrupt your work.
嗨，大衛。我希望我沒有打擾你工作。

C No, you didn't. I'm just ready for work.
不會，你沒有。我正準備要工作。

關鍵單字

▶ interrupt 打擾、妨礙、中斷
▶ ready for 準備好做某事

Chapter 18

結束通話

【Unit 01】結束通話

I got to hang up the phone.
我要掛電話了。

實用會話

A
So I really dislike my boyfriend's roommate.
所以我真的不喜歡我男朋友的室友。

B
Hmm...
嗯…

A
She's so mean to him.
她對他很壞。

B
Hmm...
嗯…

A
Are you listening to me, Jack?
傑克！你有沒有在聽我説話？

B
Yes, I am. Hey Kate, I got to hang up the phone. I'm going to be late for school.
我有。嘿，凱特，我要掛電話了，我上學快遲到了。

關鍵單字

▶ dislike　不喜歡、討厭
▶ boyfriend　男朋友
▶ roommate　住在同室的人、室友、同居者
▶ hang up　掛斷電話

【Unit 02】感謝來電

Thank you for calling me so soon.
謝謝你這麼快就打電話來。

實用會話

A
So we still have to talk about it more often.
所以我們還是需要經常討論。

B
That's right.
沒錯。

A
Do you think that Jack realizes our plans?
你認為傑克瞭解我們的計畫嗎？

B
I don't think so. We'd better tell him the whole plan.
我不這麼認為。我們最好告訴他整個計畫。

A
Definitely. Anyway, thank you for calling me so soon.
那是一定的。總之，謝謝你這麼快就打電話來。

B
Sure.
不客氣。

相關用語

▶Thank you for returning my call.
謝謝你回我電話。

▶Thank you for calling me back.
謝謝你打電話給我。

關鍵單字

▶ more often　更經常

▶ realize　完全認知、領悟、瞭解

▶ whole　整個的、全部的

▶ definitely　確實、完全(正確等)

▶ anyway　總之、總而言之

【Unit 03】很高興能和對方通話

> # Nice talking to you.
> 很高興和你通話。

實用會話

A
You know what?
你知道嗎？

B
What?
什麼？

A
I can't meet with you tomorrow.
我明天不能和你見面。

B
Why? I'm looking forward to this meeting.
為什麼？我很期待這次的會面。

A
My parents are coming to visit me tomorrow.
I have to meet them at the airport.
明天我父母要來探望我，我要去接機。

B
I see. That's OK. Nice talking to you. I've got to leave now.
我瞭解了，沒關係。很高興和你說話，我得掛電話了。

關鍵單字

▶ look forward to　期待、盼望
▶ parents　父母
▶ leave　離開(此為掛掉電話之意)

【Unit 04】必須要掛電話

> # I have to get going now.
> 我現在得要掛電話了。

實用會話

A
The doorbell is ringing. Wait a moment, please.
門鈴在響,請等一下。

B
Go answer it.
去應門吧!

(稍後)

A
I have to get going now.
我現在得要掛電話了。

B
What happened?
什麼事?

A
It's my husband. He is back.
是我先生,他回來了。

B
OK. Give me a call tomorrow.
好吧!明天打電話給我吧。

A
I will.
我會的!

關鍵單字

▶ go answer it 去回答、去應門
▶ give someone a call 打電話給某人

225

【Unit 05】準備要掛電話

I'd better get off the phone.
我得掛電話了。

實用會話

A Why don't you just tell her the truth?
你為什麼不乾脆告訴她實話？

B I will. I'm still waiting for the good opportunity.
我會的。我還在等好的機會

A All right, if you insist.
好吧，如果你堅持的話。

B I'd better get off the phone.
我必須掛電話了。

A Is she back in?
她回來了嗎？

B Yes. Bye.
對。再見。

關鍵單字

▶ opportunity 機會、時機

▶ insist 堅持、力主、非要～不可、強調、強迫

【Unit 06】歡迎對方隨時來電

> # You can call me anytime.
> 歡迎隨時打電話給我。

實用會話

A Hey, Kate, my pillow is calling me now.
嘿,凱特,我想睡覺了。

B I'll let you go for now. It's really nice talking to you.
我現在讓你掛電話。和你聊天真開心。

A Yeah, you can call me anytime.
是啊!你可以隨時打電話給我。

B Really? How nice you are.
真的?你真好。

A Sure. I'm your big brother, right?
當然,誰叫我是你的大哥,對吧?

B OK, good night.
好吧!晚安。

相關用語

▶Hey, call me when you have a chance.
嘿,有機會的話要打電話給我。

▶Try to call me when you have a chance, OK?
如果你有機會的話,試著打電話給我,好嗎?

關鍵單字

▶good night 再見、晚安 (晚上分別時用語)

【Unit 07】婉轉地結束通話

I'll let you go now.
我現在先讓你掛電話。

實用會話

A I hope I didn't bother you.
希望我沒有麻煩你。

B Don't say that. I enjoy talking to you.
不要這麼說，我很喜歡和你說話。

A It's pretty late now. I'll let you go for now.
現在很晚了，我現在先讓你掛電話。

B OK. Just give me a call when you have a chance.
好，有空要打電話給我。

A I will.
我會的。

B Bye.
再見。

關鍵單字

▶ bother 擾、打擾、迷惑、把～弄糊塗、使不安
▶ I'll let you go 我讓你走(此為讓對方掛掉電話之意)
▶ for now 現在、目前
▶ chance 機會

【Unit 08】不直接說再見地結束通話

> ### Talk to you soon.
> 再聊囉！

實用會話

A
So, this is my idea. What do you think of it?

所以這就是我的想法！你覺得如何？

B
It sounds OK. It'll change my mind.

聽起來不錯！會改變我的想法。

A
Great. Look, it's pretty now. I've got to go.

很好！哇，有點晚了！我要掛電話囉！

B
Sure. Talk to you soon.

好啊！再聊囉！

A
Bye.

再見！

相關用語

▶ I'll talk to you later.

我們再聊囉！

【Unit 09】要求親自會談

> ### Call me next week so we can talk in person.
>
> 下星期打個電話給我，我們才能見面談一談。

實用會話

A
It's pretty late now. I've to go to bed.
有點晚了！我要去睡了！

B
Yeah, it's time for bed. Call me next week so we can talk in person.
是啊，是該睡覺了！下星期打個電話給我，我們才能見面談一談。

A
I will.
我會的！

B
Great. Good night.
很好！晚安！

A
Good night.
晚安！

【Unit 10】掛對方的電話

> ### How dare you hang up on me?
> 你居然敢掛我電話？

實用會話

A Are you mad at me, honey?
親愛的，你在生我的氣嗎？

B Yes, I am.
對，我是(在生氣)。

A Why? Did I say something wrong?
為什麼？我說錯什麼了嗎？

B How dare you hang up on me yesterday?
你昨天居然敢掛我電話？

A What? Just because of that? It was an accident.
什麼？只是因為這個？那是意外。

B I don't think so.
我不這麼認為。

相關用語

▶Don't hang up.

不要掛電話。

▶Don't hang up on me.

不要掛我的電話。

關鍵單字

▶ mad at　生某人的氣
▶ dare　敢、膽敢(做...)

Chapter 19

電話相關用語

【Unit 01】接了很多通電話

> # I got a lot of calls at work today.
> 我今天在公司接好多通電話。

實用會話

A
Mark, it's your phone call from your client.
馬克,你的客戶打電話來。

B
Again?
又來了?

A
Why? You are so surprised!
怎麼了?你很訝異喔!

B
Because I got a lot of calls at work today.
因為我今天在公司接了好多通電話。

A
It's a busy day, isn't it?
今天很忙對不對?

B
Yeah, that's why I didn't have lunch yet.
對啊!這就是為什麼我還沒吃午飯。

關鍵單字

▶ client 顧客、主顧
▶ surprised 吃驚、驚奇、感到意外
▶ a lot of 很多、數量很大
▶ yet 尚未

【Unit 02】親自接電話

> # I'll get it.
> 我來接。

實用會話

（鈴聲響）

A Anybody answer the phone?
有誰可以接電話嗎？

B I'm doing the dishes right now.
我正在洗碗。

A David?
你呢，大衛？

C I'll get it, mom.
媽咪，我來接。

相關用語

▶Don't answer the phone.

不要接電話！

【Unit 03】請求代接電話

Would you answer the phone?
你可以接電話嗎？

實用會話

（電話聲響起）

A
Hello? Anybody answer the phone? Cathy?
有人嗎？有誰可以接電話？凱西？

B
Why me? I'm doing the dishes.
我什麼是我？我正在洗盤子。

A
David? Would you answer it?
大衛？你可以接電話嗎？

C
What? I can't. I'm on another line.
什麼？我不能。我正在講另一支電話。

A
Anybody there? Just pick it up.
有誰在那裡？只要把電話接起來！

D
I'll get it.
我來接。

關鍵單字

▶ do the dishes　洗盤子

▶ pick it up　接起(電話)、拿起(物品)

▶ get　接(電話)

【Unit 04】借用電話

May I use the phone?
我可以借用電話嗎？

實用會話

A Excuse me. Is Mr. Johnson in?
對不起，強生先生在嗎？

B Mr. Johnson is out of town.
強生先生出城了。

A Oh, no.
喔，糟糕。

B You have to meet him by appointment.
你想會見他，一定要預約時間。

A May I use the phone, please?
我可以借用電話嗎？

B Sure. It's over here.
當然可以。在這裡。

關鍵單字

► out of town　出城
► appointment　會面時地點的約定、預約
► use　使用

【Unit 05】撥打外線

We dial "0" first.

我們要先撥「0」。

實用會話

A Excuse me, can I use your phone?
　抱歉，我可以借用你的電話嗎？

B No problem. Here you are.
　沒問題，在這裡。

A Hmm...how do I call out from your office?
　嗯…我要怎麼從你們公司撥打外線？

B We dial "0" first.
　我們都先撥「0」。

A Oh, I see. Thank you very much.
　喔，我了解了，非常謝謝你。

B Sure thing.
　小事一樁。

關鍵單字

▶ here you are　給你、在這裡
▶ call out　撥電話出去、向外打電話
▶ first　首先的、第一的、第一位的

【Unit 06】在飯店撥外線

How do I call a number outside this hotel?

我要怎麼從飯店撥外線出去？

實用會話

A Operator.
這是總機。

B Operator, how do I call a number outside this hotel?
總機，我要怎麼從飯店撥外線出去？

A Dial "0" first, and then the phone number.
先撥「0」再撥電話號碼。

B I see. Thank you.
我了解了，謝謝你。

A You are welcome, sir. Have a nice day.
不客氣.，先生。祝你今天愉快！

B You too. Bye.
你也是，再見。

關鍵單字

▶ outside　在～之外

【Unit 07】通話中斷線

> # I was cut off.
>
> 我電話講一半就被切斷了。

實用會話

A Hello?
喂？

(再撥一次電話)

A Hello, Emily. Sorry for that.
哈囉，艾蜜莉，剛剛對不起啦！

B What happened?
怎麼了？

A I don't know for sure. I was cut off.
我不確定。我電話講一半就被切斷了。

B That's strange.
真奇怪！

A Never mind. Where was I?
不要放心上。我説到哪兒？

B You were talking about the wedding.
你剛剛在説婚禮的事。

關鍵單字

► cut off 打斷(通話等)、使中止通話

► never mind 不要在意、不要放在心上

► wedding 結婚、婚禮

Chapter 20

電信服務

【Unit 01】安裝電話申請

> **I'd like to have a phone installed.**
> 我要安裝電話。

實用會話

A I'd like to have a phone installed.
我要安裝電話。

B May I have your name and address, please?
請告訴我你的名字和地址。

A Sure. My name is Sean Brown. My address is 45 Avenue, Apartment 6.
好的,我的名字是西恩・布朗,我的地址是四十五街六號公寓。

B May I have your date of birth and your Social Security Number, please?
請告訴我你的生日和社會福利號碼。

A My date of birth is September 20, 1971. My Social Security Number is 554-66-9980.
我的生日是一九七一年九月廿日,我的社會福利號碼是 554-66-9980.

B Thank you very much. The earliest day for connection is this Friday. Is that OK?
謝謝你,安裝連線最快在這個星期五,可以嗎?

A Sure. Thanks.
可以!謝謝囉!

關鍵單字

▶ install　安裝、設置、裝置
▶ address　地址
▶ avenue　大街、通路、道路、街
▶ apartment　公寓、一套公寓房間
▶ date of birth　生日日期

【Unit 02】申請取消電話

I'd like to have my phone disconnected.

我要申請電話中止。

實用會話

A I'd like to have my phone disconnected.
我要申請取消電話。

B All right. May I have your phone number and the name on the account, please?
好的,請給我你的電話號碼和帳戶的名字。

A My name is Jeff White and phone number is 86473663.
我的名字是傑夫・懷特,電話號碼是 86473663。

B When would you like it to be disconnected?
你想要什麼時候取消電話線路?

A Tomorrow by 5:00 P.M.
明天下午五點鐘以前。

B Sure. The telephone will be disconnected at 5:00 P.M. tomorrow.
好的,電話會在明天下午五點鐘斷線。

關鍵單字

▶ account 計算、帳單、結算帳單

【Unit 03】免付費電話

> ## They have a toll-free number.
> 他們有免付費電話號碼。

實用會話

A　What's the number for information in Taiwan?
台灣的查號台是幾號？

B　It's 104. What number do you need?
是104。你要查什麼電話？

A　I want to call Pink Restaurant.
我要打電話到「粉紅餐廳」。

B　They have a toll-free number. It's 0800 568912.
他們有免付費電話號碼，是0800568912。

A　I had better call them to make a reservation right now. Thanks a lot!
我最好現在打個電話去預約，多謝啦！

B　You are welcome.
不客氣。

關鍵單字

► information　資訊、訊息、情報
► need　需要、需求
► a toll-free number　免付費電話號碼
► make a reservation　預約

【Unit 04】在飯店早上叫醒服務

I'd like to have a wake-up call at 8 A.M.

我要設定早上八點鐘的電話鬧鈴服務。

實用會話

A Can I have a morning call tomorrow?
我能設定明天早上電話鬧鈴嗎？

B Of course you can. What time do you want?
當然可以。你想要什麼時間（叫醒）？

A I'd like to have a wake-up call at 8 A.M.
我要設定早上八點鐘的電話鬧鈴服務。

B OK. We will call you at 8 o'clock tomorrow
好的，我們明天會在八點鐘打電話給你。

A And I'd like a wake-up call every morning.
而且我每一天都要早上叫醒(的服務)。

B No problem, sir.
沒問題的，先生。

關鍵單字

▶ morning call 早晨叫醒
▶ wake-up call 叫起床的電話

Part

3

職場情境短語

Chapter 1

辦公室電話用語

接起電話先問候

A
Good afternoon, this is Sarah Jones speaking. How may I help you?
午安！我是莎拉·瓊斯。有什麼需要我效勞的嗎？

B
Hi, I'm looking for the manager of sales.
嗨，我要找你們的銷售部門的經理。

接起電話表明身份

A
Hi, may I speak to Mr. Smith?
嗨，我要找史密斯先生。

B
This is he. What can I do for you?
我就是！有什麼我可以協助的嗎？

去電找人

A
Can you put Mr. Brown on the phone?
請布朗先生來聽電話好嗎？

B
Hold on a second.
請稍等！

相關用語
▶ I need to talk to your supervisor.
我要和你的主管說話。

去電表明身份和公司

A This is David Baker from T&T Company.
我是T&T公司的大衛・貝克。

B What can I do for you, Mr. Baker?
貝克先生,有什麼我可以協助的嗎?

去電請求協助

A Hi, I had some problem with my orders. I was wondering if you could help me out.
嗨,我的訂單有一些問題。我在想你能不能幫我解決。

B Sure. May I have your name, please?
可以刀的!請問你的大名?

幫來電者轉接來電

A May I speak to Mr. Baker, please?
請找貝克先生聽電話。

B I'll transfer this call to Mr. Baker's office.
我幫你把電話轉到貝克先生的辦公室。

職務已經轉換

A May I speak to Mr. Brown, please?
請找布朗先生聽電話。

B He doesn't work for this department anymore.
他現在沒有在這個部門服務了！

職務負責人

A Who is taking over from Mr. Brown?
誰接替布朗先生的職務？

B It's John Baker. I'll transfer you to him.
是約翰・貝克。我幫你把電話轉給他。

相關用語

▶ Who is in charge here?
這裡由誰負責？

仍在忙線中

A Hi, David. Got a minute to talk now?
嗨，大衛！你現在有空聊一聊嗎？

B Now? No. I'm on another line now.
現在？沒有耶！我現在正在忙線中。

要求對方打電話

A Give me a call at work.
　上班的時候打電話給我。

B Sure.
　好的！

相關用語

▶ Give me a call at any time.
隨時都可以打電話給我！

又再次來電

A Hello?
　喂？

B Hi, David, it's John again.
　嗨，大衛，又是我約翰！

告知自己的聯絡方式

A Does he know your phone number?
　他知道你的電話號碼嗎？

B I can be reached at 86473663 or 0900123456.
　可以打電話到86473663或0900123456聯絡到我。

用電話安排會議

A
Hello?

喂？

B
Hi, David. We'll have to arrange a meeting. Have a look at your schedule and call me back.

嗨，大衛！我們要安排會議。你看看你的行程後再打電話給我。

詢問是否可以參加會議

A
Can you attend the meeting?

你能參加會議嗎？

B
Nope. I'm swamped with work at the moment.

不能耶！我現在工作很多。

時間是否方便

A
What time would be good for you?

你什麼時候有空？

B
How about this Friday?

這個星期五如何？

因為太忙無法開會

A Can we have a meeting this morning?
我們今天早上可以開會嗎？

B This morning? Sorry, I'm quite busy this morning.
今天早上？抱歉，我今天早上很忙！

已經安排行程

A How about 2 pm?
下午兩點鐘如何？

B I don't think so. I have something scheduled.
恐怕不行！我已經安排好行程了！

敲定會面的時間

A I was hoping to set up an appointment with you for sometime this week.
我想要本週和你約個時間會面。

B How about this Wednesday?
要不要就這個星期三？

本週都很忙

A I'm pretty booked up this week.

我這個星期都很忙。

B Let's move it up to next week. What do you say?

那就移到下個星期。你覺得呢？

先做確認

A Let me take a look. All right, that's no problem.

我看一下！好的！沒有問題。

B Great. See you then.

很好！到時候見囉！

明天請假

A How about tomorrow?

明天呢？

B Nope. I'm taking the day off tomorrow.

不行！我明天請假！

抱怨太忙

A
I got so much work to do this week.
我這個星期有好多工作要做！

B
You should take a day off.
你應該要放個假！

受話方會回來的時間

A
Is Mr. Brown there?
布朗先生在嗎？

B
No. He'll be here at about two.
不在！他要到兩點鐘才會回來！

請同事協助提供諮詢

A
Hi, David. There is something I'd like to consult with you.
嗨，大衛！我有些事想要請教你！

B
Go ahead.
請說吧！

相關用語

▶I need your help.

我需要你的協助！

▶Please help me out.

請幫幫我！

客戶在線上

A Kate, there's a David on the phone asking for an appointment.

凱特，線上有一位大衛要詢問預約的事。

B OK. Put him through.

好的！轉接過來！

轉接電話給同事

A Jenny, it's Kate. She wants to talk with you.

珍妮，是凱特。他想要和你通話。

B All right. Just put her through, thanks.

好的！轉接過來，謝謝。

相關用語

▶There's a David on line 2.

二線電話有一位大衛待接通。

提供幫助

A Let me write down your requests.
我來記下你的需求。

B OK. Call me back in a minute.
好的，馬上回我電話。

相關用語

►Don't worry about it.
不用擔心！

為所引起的不便致歉

A I'm sorry for the inconvenience.
抱歉我所引起的不便。

B Come on. It's OK.
別這樣，沒關係啦！

打電話到其他部門

A Hello, is this Maintenance Department?
哈囉，是維修部門嗎？

B Yeah. That's right. What can I do for you?
是的，沒錯。可以為你服務嗎？

答應支援

A Could you come and take a look at it?
你可以來檢查一下嗎？

B Let me see. OK, I'll be there about two.
我瞧瞧！好的！我兩點鐘過去。

剛剛和誰通電話

A Who called just now?
剛剛是誰打電話過來？

B I'm not sure. The number doesn't look familiar.
我不太清楚。電話號碼很陌生。

回覆對方先前的來電

A Hello?
喂？

B Hi, John. I'm returning your call.
嗨，約翰。我回你電話。

相關用語

▶ I heard your message.
我有聽到你的留言。

會再回電給對方

A I'll call you.
　我會打電話給你。

B OK. I'll be waiting.
　好的,我等你電話。

相關用語

▶ I'll be back in a minute.

　我馬上回來。

▶ I'll call you back.

　我會再回電給你。

會再通知對方

A I'll let you know.
　我會再通知你。

B Thanks a lot.
　多謝啦!

感謝來電

A Thank you for calling.
　感謝來電。

B Sure.
　不客氣。

很高興和對方通話

A It's nice talking to you.
很高興和你通電話。

B Yes, it is.
是啊！的確是！

相關用語

▶ Nice talking to you.

很高興和你通電話。

結束通話

A See you then. Have a nice day.
再見囉！祝你今天愉快！

B You, too.
你也是！

相關用語

▶ I'll talk to you later.

再見囉！

▶ Good-bye.

再見！

Chapter 2

秘書電話用語

幫老闆接電話

A Good morning. You have reached the office of Mr. Jones.
早安！這是瓊斯先生的辦公室。

B Hello. Can I speak to Chris?
喂！我要找克里斯接電話。

相關用語

▶ Good morning. This is China Airlines.
早安。這是中華航空公司。

▶ How may I help you?
需要我協助嗎？

▶ T&B Company. May I help you?
這是T&B 公司。可以為你服務嗎？

打電話找人

A May I speak to David or John, please?
我可以和大衛或是約翰講話嗎？

B They're not here. Can I give them a message?
他們不在這裡。要留言給他們嗎？

請問來電者身份

A Who is speaking, please?
請問你是哪一位？

B This is David White.
我是大衛‧懷特。

相關用語

► Who is this?

你是哪一位？

► Who is this, please?

請問你是哪一位？

► Who is calling, please?

請問你是哪一位？

請問來電者的姓名

A What did you say your name was, please?
你說你的大名是？

B This is David calling from New York.
我是從紐約打電話來的大衛。

相關用語

► May I ask who is calling, please?

我能知道你的姓名嗎？

▶ Who should I say is calling?

我應該要説是誰來電？

▶ May I tell him who is calling?

需要我告訴他是誰來電嗎？

▶ May I have your last name, please?

請問你貴姓？

▶ Hi, this is Neil with Apple Design.

嗨，我是蘋果設計的尼爾。

▶ Hi, this is David from IBM.

嗨，我是IBM的大衛。

▶ Hello, this is David with IBM Company.

哈囉，我是IBM公司的大衛。

Tip 5

代為確認受話方是否在

A　I'd like to speak to Mr. Hudson, please.

我要和哈德森先生説話。

B　Let me see if he is available.

我看看他現在有沒有空。

相關用語

▶ Let me see if he is in.

我看看他在不在。

▶ Let me take a look for you.

我幫你看一看。

► Let me see for you if he is in.

我幫你看一看他在不在。

► I will find out if Mr. Hudson is in his office.

我看看哈德森先生在不在他的辦公室。

老闆不在座位上

A Is Mr. Hudson around?

哈德森先生在嗎？

B I'm sorry, but he is not at his desk now.

很抱歉，他現在不在座位上。

相關用語

► He is not in his seat.

他不在座位上。

► He just stepped away.

他剛剛走開了。

► I am afraid he is not here.

他恐怕不在這裡。

老闆暫時離座了

A Hello, may I speak to Mr. Hudson, please?
哈囉,我能和哈德森先生説話嗎?

B He just went out.
他剛剛才離開。

相關用語

►He is out now.
他現在出去了。

►Mr. Hudson just stepped out.
哈德森先生剛剛離開了。

►I'm afraid he's out at the moment.
他現在恐怕不在這裡。

►I'm sorry that he's not in his office now.
很抱歉,他現在不在他的辦公室。

老闆短期內不進公司

A Is Mr. Hudson in his office?
哈德森先生有在他的辦公室嗎?

B He won't be back until this Friday.
他本週五前不會回來。

相關用語

▶Mr. Hudson is not in now.

哈德森先生現在不在（公司）。

▶Mr. Hudson is out of town.

哈德森先生出城去了。

▶Mr. Hudson will return to the office after lunch.

哈德森先生會在午餐後回到辦公室。

老闆正在忙無法接電話

A Is Mr. Hudson in today?

哈德森先生今天在嗎？

B I'm sorry, but he is in a meeting right now.

很抱歉，他現在正在開會中。

相關用語

▶Mr. Hudson is not available at the moment.

哈德森先生現在沒有空。

▶I'm afraid Mr. Hudson won't be free until three o'clock.

恐怕哈德森先生三點鐘前都不會有空。

▶Mr. Hudson is in a meeting with Mr. Jones at the moment.

哈德森先生和瓊斯先生正在開會中。

老闆正在電話忙線中

A
Is he off the line?

他講完電話了嗎？

B
Sorry, sir. His line is busy now.

抱歉，先生。他在忙線中。

相關用語

▶The line is busy.

電話佔線中。

▶He's busy with another line.

他現在正在忙線中。

▶He's on another line now.

他現在正在講另一通電話。

▶He's talking to someone else now.

他現在正和其他人在講話。

▶I'm sorry, but he's busy with another line.

很抱歉，他正在講另一通電話。

▶I'm sorry, but he's tied up at the moment.

很抱歉，他現在正忙。

預估老闆回來的時間

A May I speak to Mr. Hudson, please?
我能和哈德森先生説話嗎？

B He won't be back until four thirty.
他要四點卅分才會回來。

相關用語

▶He said he'd be back before three.

他説他三點鐘前會回來。

▶He'd be here around five o'clock.

他大約五點鐘會回來。

提供來電者協助

A He isn't in. Maybe I can be of assistance.
他不在，也許我可以提供協助。

B All right. Please ask him to return my call.
好吧！請他回我電話。

相關用語

▶Do you want to speak to someone else?

你要和其他人講電話嗎？

老闆剛回座

A
I'd like to speak to Mr. Hudson, please.
我要和哈德森先生説話。

B
Oh, he just came back.
喔，他剛好回來了。

詢問對方是否要留言

A
Would you like to leave a message?
你要留言嗎？

B
Sure. Would you tell Mr. Hudson that I called?

好的！能請你告訴哈德森先生我來電過嗎？

相關用語

▶Would you care to leave a message?

你要留言嗎？

▶Do you have any messages?

你有任何留言嗎？

▶Could you leave a message?

你要留言（給他）嗎？

▶Do you want to leave a message?

你要留言嗎？

▶He's not in. May I take a message for him?

他不在。我能幫他留言嗎？

請對方轉達自己在找受話方

A Can you let him know that I am looking for him?

能不能請你告訴他我在找他？

B I'll tell him you called.

我會告訴他你有打電話來就可以了。

相關用語

▶ Just let him know I called.

只要讓他知道我有打電話來。

去電要求留言

A May I speak to Mr. Hudson?

我能和哈德森先生講電話嗎？

B He left for New York on business yesterday.

他先生昨天就到紐約去出差了。

A Could I leave him a message?

我能留言給他嗎？

相關用語

▶ Could you give him a message, please?

你能幫我留話給他嗎？

271

記下留言

A
Please ask him to return my call.
請他回我電話。

B
Let me get this down.
讓我寫下來。

相關用語

▶I think I have got it all down.

我全寫下來了。

確認留言內容

A
Let me make sure I got it all right.
我確認一下是否都寫對。

B
No problem.
沒問題！

相關用語

▶Is this message correct?

留言對嗎？

▶Let me read this back to you.

我再複誦一遍。

▶Could you repeat that again?

你能再説一次嗎？

▶Slow down, please.

請(説)慢一點。

確認對方的電話號碼

A
Let me leave my number in case he lost it.
我留我的電話,以免他丟了(我的電話)。

B
Is that Chris at 0900111222?
是克里斯,電話0900111222嗎?

相關用語

►What number can he reach you at?

他可以打哪個電話號碼給你?

請求回電

A
Do you want to leave a message?
你要留言嗎?

B
This is Nancy. Tell him to call me back.
這是南西來電!告訴他回我電話。

相關用語

►Would you ask him to call Mr. Smith back?

能請他回史密斯先生的電話嗎?

►Please ask him to call Mr. Smith back later.

請他晚一點回史密斯先生的電話。

►Would you have him call me back?

能請你轉告他回我電話嗎?

►Tell him to call me back as soon as possible.

告訴他盡快回我電話。

►Would you please tell him to call back this afternoon?

請你告訴他今天下午回個電話好嗎？

去電請對方轉接分機

A　Extension 403, please.
　　請接分機403。

B　Wait a moment, please.
　　請稍等！

相關用語

►Please connect me with extension 403.

請幫我接分機403。

►Could I have extension number 403?

可以幫我轉接分機403嗎？

►May I have extension 403?

可以幫我轉接分機403嗎？

►Would you please transfer this call to extension 403?

能請你(幫我)將電話轉接給分機403嗎？

告知會再來電

A Would you like to talk to someone else?
你要和其他人講電話嗎？

B No, thanks. I'll call back later.
不用，謝謝！我晚一點再打來。

相關用語

▶ I'll try calling later.

我會試著晚一點再打來。

▶ I'll try another time.

我會在其他時候再試試。

▶ I'll try again later.

我等一下再打來。

▶ I'll call him by five.

我五點鐘再打電話給他。

先接插撥電話

A Can you hang on a second? I have got a call.
你能等一下嗎？我接個電話。

B Sure.
好啊！

相關用語

► I have call waiting on my phone.

我有一通插撥電話待接。

► Hold on a second. I got to answer another phone call.

請稍候，我要先接另一線電話。

► I'll be right back.

我會馬上回來（和你通電話）。

代為轉接電話

A Do you need me to direct your call?

需要我幫你轉接過去嗎？

B Yes, please.

好的！麻煩你囉！

相關用語

► I'll put you through.

我幫你接過去。

► I'll transfer you to the sales department.

我會把你的電話轉到行銷部門。

► I'll connect you.

我幫你轉接電話。

► I'll get him to the phone.

我請他來接電話。

老闆詢問是否有留言

A Any messages for me?
有沒有我的留言？

B You have two new messages.
你有兩則新留言。

告知老闆有來電待接

A It's David.
是大衛（打電話來）。

B Put him through.
把他轉接接過來。

相關用語

▶Mr. Hudson, it's for you.
哈德森先生，找你的（電話）。

▶It's for you.
找你的（電話）

▶Your phone.
(有)你的電話。

告知老闆有特定人士來電

A Mr. Hudson, Dr. Jones is on line four.
哈德森先生，瓊斯博士在四線。

B I told you to hold all calls for me.
我有告訴過你幫我留話啊！

告知老闆有緊急電話待接

A David is on line two. He says it's urgent.
大衛在二線電話上。他說有急事。

B Put him through.
把他轉接接過來。

告知老闆有誰來電

A Who called just now?
剛才誰打電話來？

B It's Mr. Smith. He wants you to return his call.
是史密斯先生。他要你回他電話。

Chapter 3

總機人員電話用語

客戶的帳單有問題

A I've got some questions about my bill.
我的帳單有一點問題！

B What about them, sir?
是什麼問題，先生？

提供資訊

A How may I help you?
有什麼需要我效勞的嗎？

B Can you tell me the address of this business?
可以告訴我貴公司的地址嗎？

解決方式

A What is my PIN Number?
我的PIN卡是幾號？

B We'll send your PIN to your e-mail account.
我們會將你的PIN（號碼）寄到你的e-mail帳號。

信用卡帳單的問題

A Hello. I have some questions about my last credit card statement.

哈囉！我有關於一些上一期信用卡帳單的問題。

B Fire away. I'll be happy to answer your questions.

請說！我很樂意為你解決問題。

打國際電話

A Good morning. How may I help you?

早安！有什麼需要我效勞的嗎？

B I want to make an overseas call.

我想要打一通國際電話。

國際電話要打到哪個國家？

A What country do you want to call?

你想要打到哪一個國家？

B Taiwan. I don't know the country code.

台灣。我不知道國家碼。

受話方付費電話

A How can I help you?
有什麼需要我協助的嗎？

B I want to make a collect call.
我想要打一通受話方付費電話。

受話方是否願意付電話費

A You've got a collect call from David. Do you accept the charges?
你有一通來自大衛撥出的受話方付費電話。你要付費嗎？

B Yes.
好的！

免付費電話

A Is this a toll free call?
這是免付費電話嗎？

B Yes, it is. You won't be charged a dime.
是的，這是！你不用負擔任何費用。

電話插撥

A Could you hang on a second? I've got a call on line 2.

你可以等一下嗎？二線上有我的電話待接。

B No problem. I'll wait.

沒問題！我可以等！

Chapter 4

警察電話用語

剛接通電話

A This is 119. How can I help you?
這是 119。有什麼需要我協助的嗎？

B There is a car accident.
有一起交通事故發生。

表明所撥是 119

A Hello, this is 119.
嗨，這是 119。

B Hello...can you hear me?
哈囉…你聽得到我嗎？

前一刻有接到來電

A Hello?
喂？

B Hello, this is 119. We just had a phone call from this location. Your name, please?
嗨，這是 119。剛剛有人從這個電話撥到 119 中心。請問你的大名？

詢問是否有人報案

A Did somebody dial 119?
有人撥打119電話嗎？

B Yes. There's a fire at my house.
是的！我家發生火災了。

相關用語

▶Don't you want to file a report?
你不要備案嗎？

▶Do you want to file a report?
你要備案嗎？

▶Do you want to report a robbery?
你要報搶案嗎？

▶Do you want to report a theft?
你是要報竊案嗎？

是否有緊急事件

A This is 119. Do you have an emergency?
這是119。是否有緊急事件？

B I need my mama back. She's not here.
We're here by ourselves.
我要找我的媽咪。他不在這裡。我們被單獨留在
這個地方。

緊急事件為何

A　What's your emergency?
　你有緊急事件嗎？

B　Please send an ambulance.
　請派一部救護車過來。

事發地點

A　What is the location of your emergency?
　緊急事件的地點在哪裡？

B　Hmm...I don't know where I am.
　嗯…我不知道我人在哪裡。

是否需要警察的協助

A　Do you need police assistance?
　你需要警察的協助嗎？

B　Yes, I cut myself and I'm bleeding really badly. How do I stop it?
　是的。我把自己割傷了，流了很多血。我要如何止血？

請來電者不要掛斷電話

A Please stay on the line. We're sending somebody over right away.
請保持電話線路暢通。我們馬上派人過去。

B I will.
我會的！

立即派人過去

A I need an ambulance. I broke my leg.
請幫我叫一部救護車。我摔斷腿了！

B OK. Just calm down. We'll send someone
out right away.
好的！請保持冷靜。我們會立即派人過去。

請報案者待在原處

A I'm at 1211 Maple Street.
我在楓葉街1211號。

B Just stay where you are, madam.
女士，請你待在原處不要動。

接受報案

A What do you want to report, sir?
先生,你要報什麼案件?

B I want to report a robbery.
我要報搶案。

詢問對方姓名

A What's your name sir?
先生,你叫什麼名字?

B My name is John Anderson.
我叫做約翰·安德森。

詢問報案原因

A What do you want to report?
你要報什麼案件?

B I've lost my bag.
我把袋子弄丟了。

相關用語

▶ I left my bag in a cab.
我把袋子遺失在計程車上。

安撫報案者

A Someone broke into my house.
有人闖進我家了。

B Calm down, madam.
女士，先冷靜下來。

發生什麼事

A What happened to you?
你怎麼啦？

B I was robbed on First Avenue yesterday.
我昨天在第一大道被搶了。

相關用語

▶ I was robbed.

我被搶劫了。

▶ My bag was snatched.

我的袋子被搶了。

▶ He snatched the money out of my hand.

他把錢從我的手裡搶走了。

人口失蹤的報案

A My kid is missing.
我的孩子失蹤了。

B Do you have any pictures of your kid?
你有孩子的照片嗎？

相關用語

▶ My wife was kidnapped.
我的太太被綁架了。

詢問是否有目擊

A Did you see that guy?
你有看到那個人嗎？

B I saw nothing.
我什麼都沒有看到。

案件發生的時間

A I was robbed.
我被搶劫了。

B When did it happen?
什麼時候發生的？

相關用語

▶What time did this happen?

這是什麼時間發生的？

▶What time did this accident occur?

這件事故是什麼時候發生的？

▶Do you remember when it happened?

你記得發生的時間嗎？

▶How long ago?

多久之前？

Tip 20 警察會接手處理所有的事

A I'm so scared.
我好害怕。

B We'll take care of everything.
我們會處理一切的。

相關用語

▶Let me take care of it.

我來處理。

▶Don't worry about it. We'll take care of everything.

別擔心，我們會處理所有的事。

Chapter 5

航空公司人員
電話用語

向航空公司預訂機位

A Do you fly from Hong Kong to Chicago next week?

你們有下星期從香港到芝加哥的班機嗎？

B Wait a moment, please. I'll see if there are any flights.

請稍等，我查一下是否有任何班機。

指定班機訂位

A I'd like to book flight 615 on August 25th.

我要訂八月廿五日的615班次班機。

B OK. May I have your name, please?

好的，請給我你的名字。

訂兩個人的機票

A I'd like to book two seats from Taipei to Hong Kong on August 25th.

我要訂兩個人八月廿五日從台北到香港的機票。

B May I have both of your names, please?

請給我你們的名字。

訂來回機票

A I'd like to book a Round-Trip ticket from Taipei to London.
我要訂一張從台北到倫敦的來回機票。

B When do you want to depart?
你想什麼時候離境？

變更班機

A United Airlines. May I help you?
聯合航空，可以為你服務嗎？

B This is John Simon calling. I'd like to change my flight.
我是約翰‧賽門，我想變更班機。

指定特定日期的班機訂位

A I'd like to book flight 615 on August 25th.
我要訂八月廿五日的615班次班機。

B OK. May I have your name, please?
好的，請給我你的名字。

電話英語 Make a phone call
一本通

詢問姓名

A How do you spell your name, please?
你的名字如何拼？

B C-H-R-I-S W-H-I-T-E.
C-H-R-I-S W-H-I-T-E。

A Thank you. I'll book it for you right now.
謝謝你，我馬上幫你訂位。

訂兩個人的機票

A I'd like to book two seats from Taipei to Hong Kong on August 25th.
我要訂兩個人八月廿五日從台北到香港的機票。

B May I have both of your names, please?
請你給我你們的名字。

訂哪一班飛機

A I'd like the 9 A.M. one.
我要九點鐘的那一班。

B There's a flight at 8 A.M. and one at 10 A.M. Which one would you prefer?
早上八點鐘有一班，另一班是十點鐘。你想要哪一班？

詢問再確認機票的資料

A I'd like to confirm a flight for Mr. Jones.
我要幫瓊斯先再確認機票。

B Certainly. What is the flight number and date of departure, please?
好的！請問班機號碼和離境的時間。

再確認機票

A It's flight 615 to New York on May 7th at 5 pm. The name is David Jones.
航班 615 號到紐約，在五月七日下午五點鐘。名字是大衛‧瓊斯。

B Thank you. Please wait a moment while I confirm the flight.
謝謝你！請稍候，我來確認班機。

Chapter 6

旅館櫃臺人員
電話用語

接起電話詢問是否需要協助

A Good afternoon. Is this Four Stars Hotel?
午安！這是四星飯店嗎？

B Yes, madam. May I help you?
是的，女士。可以為你服務嗎？

詢問要單人房或是雙人房

A I'd like to make a reservation for three nights.
我要預約三晚住宿。

B All right. Single or double room?
好的！要單人房還是雙人房？

房客住房的天數

A How many nights will you be staying?
你打算住房幾天？

B Three nights. It's from Monday to Wednesday.
三天！從星期一到星期三。

房客何時抵達飯店

A I need to make a reservation for Mr. Jones.
我要幫瓊斯先生預約。

B When will Mr. Jones be arriving?
瓊斯先生何時會抵達？

A He'll be there next Friday.
他會在下週五抵達。

詢問名字的拼法

A How do you spell the last name, please?
請問你的姓氏怎麼拼？

B V-A-L-E.
是 V-A-L-E。

聽不清楚某些字

A Did you say "B" or "V"?
你是說 B 還是 V？

B "V" as in "Victory."
Victory 的 V。

說明收費

A How much does it charge?
這要收多少錢？

B It's NT$800. We'll charge you when you check out.
要台幣八百元。我們會在你退房時收費。

表明是客房服務中心

A Room service.
(這裡是)客房服務中心。

B Our hair dryer is broken.
我們的吹風機壞了。

需要何種服務

A Customer Service Center, may I help you?
客戶服務中心，你好，需要我的協助嗎？

B I'd like to order room service, please.
我要食物送到房間的服務。

有提供的服務

A Room service.
(這裡是)客房服務中心。

B Do you have laundry service?
你們有衣物送洗的服務嗎？

A Yes, we do, sir.
先生，我們有(這項服務)。

點什麼客房服務餐點

A What do you want to order?
你想要點什麼？

B Would you bring us a bottle of champagne?
你能帶一瓶香檳給我們嗎？

是否要其他服務

A What else do you want, sir?
先生，你還需要其他的東西嗎？

B Let's see, and I want a chicken sandwich.
我想想，還有我要一份雞肉三明治。

詢問發生什麼問題

A What's the matter with it?
發生什麼問題？

B I don't know. It's not working anymore.
我不知道！就不能運作啦！

替房客安排事宜

A Customer Service Center. How may I be of help?
客戶服務中心，你好。需要我的協助嗎？

B Yes, I'd like an extra cot for Room 604.
是的，我要在604房多加一張床。

A Yes, sir. We'll arrange it for you right away.
好的，先生。我們會盡快為你安排。

馬上執行

A I'm going to catch my train. Could you make it quickly?
我要趕火車。你能快一點嗎？

B No problem, sir. We'll do it right now.
先生，沒問題的。我們馬上(派人)去做。

馬上派人員過去

A Can you please hurry?
你能快一點嗎？

B OK. We'll send someone to fix it right away.
好的。我們會馬上派人過去。

五分鐘內馬上派人員過去

A I can't find any towels in my room. Can you send someone up to have a look?
我房間裡沒有毛巾！可以請你派個人上來瞧一瞧嗎？

B Yes, madam. We'll be there in five minutes.
好的，女士！五分鐘內就會有人過去。

告知如何抵達飯店

A How can I get to your hotel from the airport?
我要如何從機場到（你們的）飯店？

B You can catch the shuttle bus outside the South Terminal, or you can take a taxi.
你可以搭乘在南方航廈的接駁公車，或是你可以搭乘計程車。

基本句型

打電話找人

當你聽到對方說～

☞ Is ⬚ (人名) around?

(人名)在嗎？

☞ Is ⬚ (人名) in?

(人名)在這裡嗎？

☞ Is ⬚ (人名) at home?

(人名)在家嗎？

☞ May I speak to ⬚ (人名), please?

哈囉，我能和~(人名)説話嗎？

你就可以回答～

☞ This is he/she.

我就是本人。

☞ This is ⬚ (人名).

我就是~(人名)。

☞ Speaking.

請説。

請來電者稍候

當你聽到對方說～

☞ Just a minute, please.

請等一下。

☞ One moment, please.

請等一下。

☞ Wait a moment, please.

請等一下。

你就可以回答～

☞ Yes.

好的。

☞ Sure

當然。

☞ No problem.

沒問題。

☞ I will hold.

我會(等)。

要找的人不在

當你聽到對方說～

☞ He/She is out.

他/她不在。

☞ He/She is not here.

他/她不在這裡。

☞ He/She is not at his/her desk.

他/她不在座位上。

☞ He/She just went out.

他/她剛出去。

你就可以繼續問～

☞ Do you know when he/she will be back?

你知道他/她什麼時候會回來嗎？

☞ When do you expect him/her back?

你預期他/她什麼時候會回來？

☞ Do you know where he/she is going?

你知道他/她去哪裡嗎？

要找的人無法接電話

當你聽到對方說～

☞ He/She is not available.

他/她現在沒有空。

☞ He/She is busy with another line.

他/她正在另一條線上（講電話）。

☞ He/She is in a meeting now.

他/她正在開會。

☞ He/She is in the middle of something.

他/她正在忙。

你就可以回答～

☞ May I leave a message?

我可以留言嗎？

☞ Have him/her call me at ☐ (電話號碼), please.

請叫他打電話到～(電話號碼)給我。

☞ Tell him/her to give me a call.

告訴他/她打電話給我。

問來電者的身份

當你聽到對方說～

☞ May I know who is calling?
我能知道你是誰嗎？

☞ Who is this?
你是哪一位？

☞ Who is speaking, please?
請問你是哪一位？

你就可以回答～

☞ This is ⬚ (人名).
我是~(人名)。

☞ This is ⬚ (人名) calling.
我是～(人名)。

☞ This is ⬚ (人名) calling for ⬚ (人名).
我是～(人名)打電話找～(人名)。

出差英文 1000 句型(附 MP3)

「出差英文寶典」明天就要出差了，該如何和外籍伙伴、客戶溝通？誰說英文不好就不能出差？只要帶著這一本，就可以讓你國外出差無往不利、攻無不克！

商業實用英文 E-mail(業務篇) 附文字光碟

最新版附實用書信文字光碟讓你寫商業 Mail 不用一分鐘 5 大例句+E-mail 商用書信實例，讓你立即寫出最完備的商用英文 E-mail。

商業實用英文 E-mail(人際) 附文字光碟

實用例句+書信實例讓您立即寫出最完美的辦公室英文 E-mail。立即學、馬上用，完整學習 step by step，讓您利用英文 E-mail 拓展人際關係。Chapter 1 實用語句範例 Chapter 2 祝賀基本用語 Chapter 3 E-mail 信函實例…

網拍學英語

英文網拍達人出列！老是看不懂英文購物網站嗎？本書 step by step，一步步教您學會網拍英文！看上了英文網拍的商品，卻不知道如何競標、下單嗎？本書每個步驟詳細解釋，讓您順利在英文網站上當個賣方或買方！

國家圖書館出版品預行編目資料

電話英語一本通/張瑜凌編著.
--初版.--臺北縣汐止市:雅典文化,民98.03
　　面;　公分.--(全民學英文系列:16)
　　ISBN:978-986-7041-75-3　(平裝附光碟片)

1. 英語　　　2. 會話

805.188　　　　　　　　　　　　　　98000543

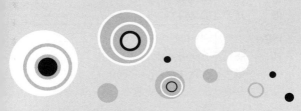

全民學英文 **16** 電話英語一本通

編　　著	張瑜凌
出 版 者	雅典文化事業有限公司
登 記 證	局版北市業字第五七〇號
發 行 人	黃玉雲
執行編輯	張瑜凌
編 輯 部	221台北縣汐止市大同路三段194-號9樓
電子郵件	a8823.a1899@msa.hinet.net
電　　話	02-86473663
傳　　真	02-86473660
郵　　撥	18965580雅典文化事業有限公司
法律顧問	永信法律事務所　林永頌律師
總 經 銷	永續圖書有限公司 221台北縣汐止市大同路三段194-號9樓
電子郵件	yungjiuh@ms45.hinet.net
郵　　撥	18669219永續圖書有限公司
網　　站	www.foreverbooks.com.tw
電　　話	02-86473663
傳　　真	02-86473660
ISBN	978-986-7041-75-3
初　　版	2009年04月
定　　價	NT\$ **169**元

ⓐ 雅典文化 **讀者回函卡**

謝謝您購買這本書。
為加強對讀者的服務，請您詳細填寫本卡，寄回**雅典文化**；
並請務必留下您的E-mail帳號，我們會主動將最近 "好康"
的促銷活動告 訴您，保證值回票價。

書　　　名：電話英語一本通
購買書店：＿＿＿＿＿＿市/縣＿＿＿＿＿＿＿＿＿書店
姓　　　名：＿＿＿＿＿＿＿＿　生　日：＿＿＿年＿＿月＿＿日
身分證字號：＿＿＿＿＿＿＿＿＿＿＿＿＿＿＿＿＿＿＿
電　　　話：(私)＿＿＿＿＿(公)＿＿＿＿＿(手機)＿＿＿＿＿
地　　　址：□□□ ＿＿＿＿＿＿＿＿＿＿＿＿＿＿＿＿
E - mail：＿＿＿＿＿＿＿＿＿＿＿＿＿＿＿＿＿＿＿
年　　　齡：□20歲以下　□21歲～30歲　□31歲～40歲
　　　　　　□41歲～50歲　□51歲以上
性　　　別：□男　□女　　婚姻：□單身　□已婚
職　　　業：□學生　　□大眾傳播　□自由業　□資訊業
　　　　　　□金融業　□銷售業　　□服務業　□教職
　　　　　　□軍警　　□製造業　　□公職　　□其他
教育程度：□高中以下（含高中）□大專　□研究所以上
職 位 別：□負責人　□高階主管　　□中級主管
　　　　　　□一般職員　□專業人員
職 務 別：□管理　　　□行銷　　□創意　　□人事、行政
　　　　　　□財務、法務　　　□生產　□工程　　□其他＿＿＿＿
您從何得知本書消息？
　　　□逛書店　　□報紙廣告　□親友介紹
　　　□出版書訊　□廣告信函　□廣播節目
　　　□電視節目　□銷售人員推薦
　　　□其他＿＿＿＿＿
您通常以何種方式購書？
　　　□逛書店　　□劃撥郵購　□電話訂購　□傳真訂購　□信用卡
　　　□團體訂購　□網路書店　□其他＿＿＿＿＿
看完本書後，您喜歡本書的理由？
　　　□內容符合期待　□文筆流暢　□具實用性　□插圖生動
　　　□版面、字體安排適當　　　□內容充實
　　　□其他＿＿＿＿＿
看完本書後，您不喜歡本書的理由？
　　　□內容不符合期待　□文筆欠佳　　□內容平平
　　　□版面、圖片、字體不適合閱讀　□觀念保守
　　　□其他＿＿＿＿＿
您的建議：
＿＿＿＿＿＿＿＿＿＿＿＿＿＿＿＿＿＿＿＿＿＿＿＿＿＿

廣　告　回　信
基隆郵局登記證
基隆廣字第 056 號

台北縣汐止市大同路三段 194 號 9 樓之 1

雅典文化事業有限公司

編輯部　收

請沿此虛線對折免貼郵票，以膠帶黏貼後寄回，謝謝！

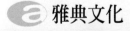

為你開啟知識之殿堂